A SUITABLE EPITAPH

Roxana Nastase

May 2017

Toronto, Canada

Toronto, Canada

ISBN: 978-1-988827-43-8

Dedication:

To Marian, for his appalling
patience

Acknowledgement:

I want to thank

Dr. James P Henley Jr

For all his help in improving the quality of this book.

It couldn't have been done without him!

A Suitable Epitaph

Klavdiya was born on the shore of a small lake in Russia forty years ago...

The woman got married in spring when the cherry trees were in blossom. She was eighteen at the time. She got divorced in autumn when the harsh rains washed the soil and the fallen leaves. She was only twenty-three and she had a young boy attached to her skirts.

...

Klavdiya died on the shore of another lake and on another continent... She'd come into the world restless and with a thirst to exceed the limitations of the world she'd been born to and she died without finding her peace.

PROLOGUE – AXEL'S VISION

The woman had been flirting with him for over fifteen minutes before he invited her to accompany him in the garden for some fresh air. Glancing out the patio doors into the darkness, she smiled. That was exactly what she'd been aiming for and she consented freely to follow him outside.

After all he was a very well built man. Maybe quite too well, she thought when she noticed him for the first time. Her mouth watered while her eyes perused the expanse of his broad shoulders and strong hands.

She needed a man. It had been some time since a man's strong hands aroused her. Probably, too long, if she considered the flutter in her belly.

The physical desire had been compelling enough, but the signs hinting to his wealth had been more important and decisive for her. The man was wealthy enough for her tastes. His suit wasn't a cheap imitation but a true Armani. She'd always had an eye for such things.

They strolled leisurely along the gravel path as she clung to his sturdy arm. He murmured some inconsequential things and she didn't bother to listen.

The power she could feel under her fingers was as exciting as the heavy smell of the roses lining the one side of the trail. She smelled romance in the air and smiled.

A few more steps and the roses made way to berry bushes. The smells changed and the heat of the summer night enveloped them in a humid cocoon.

The shingle path disappeared and she stumbled when her foot stepped on cracked soil. Both chuckled although embarrassment powdered her cheeks with a slight blush. He silently provided more support to her and a giddy feeling bubbled in her veins.

When he hastened his steps, she giggled softly and commented playfully on his haste. He was watching the trees, distracted, and didn't give any sign that he'd heard.

That determined her to bring a halt to their fast advancement through the garden. It might have been romantic, yet it didn't seem very wise. She was alone with a man she'd just met and didn't know anything about him.

It was her first time there and she hadn't been aware that the garden grounds were so extensive and secluded. Besides, while she had all intentions to flirt with him, she didn't have any intentions to succumb to his charms that night.

It was never a good idea to give in too soon. She wanted much more than a tumble in the hay and that meant that she had to play hard to get for a while. Men liked the hunt. They enjoyed the scent of their prey and the efforts that came with their chase.

The huge man glanced at her. His eyes showed understanding and he allowed her to move at a slower pace. She was wearing stilettoes and her feet thanked him. When she put on her high heels that evening before the party, she hadn't meant to wear them on that hard ground.

Once they were about forty meters away from the house and in the shadow of the trees lining that side of the garden, the man grabbed her arm and nudged her to a deserted corner. He put enough strength behind his action and the brutal move startled her.

A shiver played on the back of her neck and sent tentacles along her spine and the back of her legs. A spine-chilling feeling replaced her light-hearted mood from before, but she didn't take it lying down.

She tried to reason with him at first. She preferred to assume that maybe he was too anxious to be alone with her and that was why his attitude changed. Her well-chosen words fell on deaf ears though, and she stopped pretending. She began to oppose him but it was as if she'd been trying to stop a river flow.

Indifferent to her pleas, he dragged her for a few more meters. She continued pleading with him because she didn't see any other solution, but her attempts failed. She replenished her efforts to fight him and tried to dig her heels in the ground, but the soil was too dry and she couldn't get any traction. She just stirred a cloud of dust that rushed to find a home in her pores.

Her legs turned to jelly and she barely kept herself upright. Something was definitely wrong with what was going on there. Both her self-confidence and sense of safety had slowly skulked away during the forced walk through the trees.

Tinges of electrical shocks ran through her arms. She panicked and tears burnt her cheeks. She felt ashamed of her weakness and tried to hold them back, but the cold fingers of fear kept squeezing her heart in an iron fist, and her breath became ragged.

Probably sick of her puny attempts to detangle herself from him, he finally stopped and moved to stand before her. Through the stream of her stubborn tears she surveyed the man's stony face with dread. The man wasn't even blinking and that disconcerted her more. He was just staring at her with dead eyes which quashed her hopes.

She tried to say something again, but now she didn't find the strength to push the sounds past her lips. Her throat refused to work and her mouth was drier than the soil she felt under the thin soles of her fancy shoes.

She glanced back to the house with renewed albeit premature expectation but the trees hid it from sight. Her lips quaked when she realized that no one could see or hear her.

A corner of the man's mouth lifted in a satisfied smirk, and that sneer was a splash of cold water over her face. Even though her anxiety was climbing and reaching new heights, she understood that what he felt for her was nothing else but contempt.

That came like a shock. Not the first that evening to be sure, but this one packed the power of a live wire and her mind scattered looking for an explanation.

She'd always been certain that men admired and even worshipped her. She'd basked in their burning glances often enough and she knew that she didn't delude herself.

She stared back at him with tired eyes. She tried to decipher what lay there behind the mask but her intuition had taken cover somewhere and didn't offer any help.

The sturdy man studied her for a few moments and then, he reached out and fisted his hand over her silk blouse. His touch brought her back to the reality which had twisted a pretend romance into a horror movie. Fear bubbled near the surface now and, as her brain scrambled the signals, she was about to burst into a hysterical laughter.

In that frozen moment, that soft blouse which caressed the curve of her breasts became the most important thing in her world. She was very proud of that top as it was one of the symbols she attached to the life she'd built for herself. She'd turned that expensive piece of silk into a tangible proof that she'd exceeded both her and other people's expectations but, more important, that she'd escaped her birth circumstances, which had confined her to the working class.

The sight of that dark and threatening hand on her precious top brought a glimmer of dread but also made her see red before her eyes.

The beefy hand jerked hard and the flimsy blouse fell apart rendered to rags. Her dismay and the pressure of her fury at the sight of her prized chemise ruined ruthlessly, pushed a warlike cry past her quivering lips.

She abandoned any rational thought and jumped the man. Her shoes found soft spots in his shins and made him grunt. Her nails targeted the handsome and ruthless face she'd admired just minutes before and left blood in their wake.

He fought her back. The slap of his backhand unbalanced her. She stumbled back and cried out again and not only because of the pain. This cry echoed the terror that had swiftly creeped into her bones and fried all her neuronal cells. The man was strong and she didn't have the ability to defend herself against that brutal show of force.

Her cry died soon, though. Another man grabbed her throat from behind and his fingers gripped her as a vise and smothered the sound.

She questioned and berated herself. In the heat of the fight she'd failed to hear the other man's steps. Still, she promised herself to go down swinging.

She tried to claw into his skin but he didn't show that he registered any kind of pain. Running on instinct only, she directed her stilettoes to his shins but she couldn't say for sure if she succeeded. His fingers burrowed harder into the delicate skin and left bruises behind that marred the flawless whiteness of her epidermis. Her air pipe constricted and the woman slid slowly into unconsciousness.

Before she blacked out, she had just enough time to feel other fingers knotted in her hair. She was beyond terror and anxiety. Her impotence overwhelmed the solitary corner of her mind that was still functioning. The last thought that passed her mind was that she couldn't buy or fight her way out of that. She'd lost the game and that was her night.

The slight flicker of life in her body just made it interesting for the men around. The third man who'd grabbed her hair, threw her on the hard ground in the shadow of a bush pregnant with red drops. Her skirt climbed up and the whiteness of the exposed skin of her legs lit the darkness.

The three of them were still looming over her. They stared at her fallen body for a few seconds.

One of the attackers smirked with satisfaction, his eyes going from her body to the red berries. The ugliness in his sneer showed that he knew that the beauty of the red fruit went hand in hand with their poison and he found it befitting the situation. The woman was about to get what she deserved. Poison deserved poison.

Axel woke up with a jerk and his half-lidded eyes surveyed the bedroom. The light of the moon reflected in the glass panels of the south wall and filled the room with shadows in the corners.

His heart pounded in his chest. For one brief but agonizing moment, he'd feared that he was there with those men, who were still staring at the woman's body, which was lying in the shadow of that bush.

Now, wide awake, he breathed deeply and closed his eyes in relief. He was still in his house.

Axel's relief was short lived. He'd scarcely closed his eyes, that he had another vision of the woman's broken body.

She was lying down on that hard and dry ground which he'd seen in his dream. Now, a monotonous rain whipped her mercilessly and washed the pattern in blood which had been painted on her body, feeding it to the dehydrated soil.

The vision was so in-depth that Axel could even see the rain drops clinging to the woman's eyelashes. The light in her eyes had dimmed at first and then vanished. The lines on her forehead had deepened and marked her passing years on her face.

A few hours earlier, that face had been flawless. Now it was marred with an x high on her left cheekbone and her features showed weariness, pain and despair.

Axel flexed his fingers and wiped his damp palms off on his thighs. Axel's visions weren't always so detailed, but there were exceptions, such as the one that he'd had that night.

When the image finally blurred, Axel exhaled in a whoosh and then breathed in deeply. He wiped his forehead and noticed that his fingers weren't as steady as he knew them.

Axel shook his head and got off his bed and tried to stand. He had to lean on the night table for a few seconds before trying his wobbly legs again.

In the usual course of events, the man wouldn't have needed help to find his bearings. Axel knew his lair as well as the back of his hand and could find his way through the rooms even if he hadn't pulled the curtains aside to have the room bathed in the light of the moon. Still, that night, he needed the support of the walls to reach the bathroom.

There, he leaned on the lavabo and stared at his reflection in the mirror. Staring didn't help though. He turned on the tap and filled his fists with cold water which he liberally splashed over his face.

When the trepidation had left his body, Axel drank a mouthful. His mouth had been dry and his tongue was almost stuck to the roof of the mouth.

It wasn't enough. He brushed his teeth and only then he left the bathroom. He started towards his terrace but hesitated. He was restive and needed something more than to just listen to the owls in the night and the sounds of the lake.

With a shrug, he turned around and left his bedroom. He needed a glass of his best whiskey to wash away the metallic taste of death which still lingered in his mouth. His toothpaste hadn't succeeded in chasing it away. He also needed to make a decision.

Axel didn't know the people in his dream, but he knew the house. He'd seen that garden before. He'd strolled around it many times in the past and knew exactly where to find that pregnant bush.

Now, he had to decide what to say to the police and how. He didn't want to reveal how he knew about the crime but they would ask and he needed to plot a strategy.

CHAPTER 1 – A SUITABLE EPITAPH

Klavdiya was born on the shore of a small lake in Russia forty years ago. The information on Leah's pad didn't show it but it was raining the day Klavdiya came into the world.

The woman got married in spring when the cherry trees were in blossom. She was eighteen at the time. She got divorced in autumn when the harsh rains washed the soil and the fallen leaves. She was only twenty-three and she had a young boy attached to her skirts.

The young woman migrated to Canada the following summer where she'd already found work in a childhood friend's company.

She raised the boy to stand on his own two feet and when he left home to follow his path, she started looking around ready for the hunt.

Finally, it was her time and she wanted a man and the money that came with him. She wouldn't give any man the time of the day unless he met her expectations. He had to be well-dressed, well-behaved and with a rich portfolio.

Klavdiya died on the shore of another lake and on another continent. Her life had completed a full circle. She'd come into the world restless and with a thirst to exceed the limitations of the world she'd been born to and she died without finding her peace.

Leah sat on her haunches and looked at the battered and broken body lying at her feet in the shadow of the bush. She thought that that was a suitable epitaph after all.

She knew that she was harsh in her judgment but what she'd sensed when she touched the lifeless body made her remember a friend's words, *'Some people are just walking calls for trouble. Most of the time, trouble eventually answers their call'*.

Leah shook her head and scolded herself. No one would ever ask for what that woman got.

She stood up and turned off the pad in her hand. Then, she glanced at the coroner who meticulously discarded the surgical gloves and cleaned his hands with disinfectant.

Why he would do that, it was beyond her comprehension. Yet, she'd watched Dr. Connelly perform the same ritual every single time he was called at the scene of a fatal event.

The detective had known him for a number of years and the doctor's little quirks never ceased to astound her. Right from the beginning of their acquaintance, he stirred her curiosity, but he also pulled at her heart.

Leah's empathic skills were highly triggered whenever she looked at that gloomy old man. She'd found out that the doc wasn't a day over sixty, yet whenever she thought of him she had the feeling she would smell an old piece of parchment. That was why she got into the habit of thinking of him as an old man.

"Any word, doc?" she asked the doctor nimbly.

Leah always asked that question. She supposed it was the force of habit. The detective was compelled to inquire even though she knew that he wouldn't answer to her. Doctor Connelly was the only coroner in the force who never hazarded to give COD before completing the post mortem.

Leah turned to him just in time to catch his scowl and a small smile lifted the right corner of her mouth. Leah knew his reactions by heart and could predict them with accuracy. She actually took joy in every one of them and even found a perverse delight in yanking his chain. His answers would always make her day.

"Detective, when I have a COD, you'll be the first informed," he sternly replied with his hawk-like eyes trained on her.

His displeasure was evident in the tight curve of his mouth. His tone might have been stern but he also had a way of dragging his words which made the interlocutor aware of the sarcasm that dripped off his words like molasses in the water.

Yet, Leah felt warmth beneath the clipped words and bestowed him with a catlike smile. Her blue-green irises intensified the effect of her smile and made her seem eerie. The doc shuddered and brusquely turned and left the scene after he barked an order to the two men waiting on the side to take the body away.

Leah glanced at Klavdiya one last time. Now, no sensation came from the body. As the last drop of warmth had left the corpse, the lingering feelings and occasional thoughts from the victim vanished as well.

Leah pictured the victim's body in her mind as a shell and it wasn't for her to take care of that shell. Her role was to vindicate the victim and bring balance back into the world.

One thing that was certain about Leah was that she had a very strong sense of responsibility and she never shrunk her duties. Her innate sense of justice had pushed her on that difficult road to her family's dismay.

Leah came from a long line of empaths. Some of them had stronger abilities than others but all of them were able to sense something and read people based on those readings.

For four generations, already, her family members numbered several psychologists and counsellors, and she'd been expected to follow in their steps. Tradition was very important for her kin. They'd hoped until the last moment and hadn't resigned until she took her oath as a policewoman.

Leah was aware that she'd been a disappointment of sorts for her folks and yet, she knew she would do the same thing all over again if she'd had to choose once more.

She'd chosen to become a detective and to keep her skills hidden. The police work was chaotic enough and she didn't need to add more suspicion and stress to her colleagues' lives.

People wouldn't react favorably if they heard that she knew how they felt and sometimes why they felt the way they did. People needed to take comfort in the knowledge that they could count on the privacy of their thoughts and feelings.

Leah might have been a disappointment to her family in the beginning, but they'd passed over their displeasure fast enough. She knew that they felt a measure of contentment because at best she hadn't chosen another line of work.

There have been cases in their clan when some of the members embraced a life of deceit and cunning. They had the skills and could pull the wool over people's eyes with ease. It wasn't a difficult career for them to pursue. All the cards were up their sleeves.

After the first three years of her career, her parents came to terms with her profession and relented in their efforts to make her change her profession. They also felt that Leah was meant to bring a sort of balance into the world and they were satisfied to see that she had a deep respect for the responsibilities they had to uphold.

CHAPTER 2 – WOMAN VS POLICEWOMAN

The policewoman walked to her car with long strides. Now that she'd finished there, she was in a hurry to get back to the office and check on a few things.

She especially wanted to verify the emergency call that told them where to find the victim. The caller described the surroundings and events with too much accuracy and that couldn't be qualified as a coincidence.

Leah was certain that the man must have witnessed everything first hand and considered the man an obvious suspect. Her palms were itching with the desire to retain him and ask him some questions.

When she opened the car door, Leah noticed that Mark, her partner, was already sprawled in the passenger seat and she grimaced. She'd been looking for him earlier but she hadn't seen him. He had a talent of making himself scarce. What astounded her was that he managed to do his job despite his sneaking and she couldn't understand how.

Mark glanced at Leah and relaxed back in his seat. His hand, which held the pad he was reading when she opened the car door, fell in his lap.

Leah noticed Mark's rebel lock of hair and a twinkle appeared in her eyes. That was so Mark. His distinctive sign, she thought. Had she been asked to describe the officer she'd have begun with that.

Mark was over thirty but that particular lock of hair made him look much younger. He'd always blow it away because it hindered his sight but it had a life of its own and stubbornly fell back on the exact same spot. Mark seemed completely unaware of his behavior. He'd done that so many times that it became a habit he couldn't shake off.

That absent-minded gesture amused Leah and yet puzzled her at the same time. The young woman failed to understand why Mark didn't merely change his haircut to get rid of the pesky lock. It was obvious that it bothered him a lot and in her book when something didn't work it was time for a change.

Leah shook her head and put the thought at rest. It wasn't for her to tell Mark what to do. She'd learned early that people disliked nothing more than unsolicited advice. Besides, they had more pressing things to discuss and she'd already wasted enough time ruminating on things with no relation to the case they had to solve. Time didn't stand still for anyone, Leah recalled.

The woman sat in her car seat and closed the door with a resounding thump. She made a weary face when she heard the sound reverberate inside the car. Leah rarely allowed her dissatisfaction to control her attitude and every slip seemed like a slap in her face.

"Tough day, boss?" Mark asked with a reluctant smile on his lips.

Leah glanced at him and noticed that he seemed unwilling to provoke a discussion or, worse, a scolding, even though Leah rarely showed her claws. That didn't mean she didn't have any. The policeman had felt those claws a few times over the years and, apparently, didn't feel like repeating the experience.

Leah cast a stern look in his direction. While it was true that she outranked him, she never got used to his calling her '*boss*'. She'd asked him to use her name several times and expected him to have learned his lesson by then. The detective was weary of reminding him about it all the time and sometimes, she wondered if he didn't do it on purpose, just to test her restraint. Yet, the strain around his eyes and the vibes that came from Mark disagreed with her assumption and she preferred to let it go.

She looked out the window and saw that the sun had already reached up in the sky, a definite sign that the morning had come to an end. A black bird, maybe a hawk or a raven, sailed above with its wings outstretched and a piercing shout followed.

Leah knew very little about birds, maybe just that they flew and ate worms. Her eyes followed the arrogant bird for a few seconds and then, her eyes swept over the people gathered about twenty paces away from the yellow band.

Leah could read a broad array of feelings from the small crowd. She felt dismay, fear, pity and there it was, smug satisfaction.

It wasn't unexpected. Despite the saying *'Never speak ill about the dead'*, there was always at least one person who disliked the dead with a passion and the satisfaction at the news of the victim's demise overrode their common sense.

Leah never frowned upon such a discovery. She understood people better than normal people did and she allowed room for such petty thoughts. She'd come to terms with the knowledge that humankind was actually anything but kind.

Still, there was something else there. The sensation was indefinite. It was just a probing tentacle which touched her mind and aroused her restlessness.

The young woman scanned the faces again carefully with the trained eyes of a police officer. At the same time, she tried to probe their minds, as well, using the skills she'd honed over many years.

A man turned his back to her slowly before her eyes could have reached him and seen his features. He started towards the house and she could see that his fists were clenched in the pockets of his white linen cotton pants. His stride was long and lazy as if he hadn't a worry in the world. Still, Leah would have bet the shirt on her back that tension defined the lines of his back muscles.

Her eyes lingered on his back and she tried to assess him objectively, yet she couldn't note anything distinctive but his curvy raven hair, which reached the collar of his white shirt, and the strong line of his shoulders. She didn't fail to notice the movement of his muscles under the loose shirt, though.

The man reminded her of an elegant and yet, ferocious feline cut loose out in the wild, absorbed in the mission of checking out its personal hunting grounds.

Leah focused on him until he disappeared behind the line of decorative trees. She hadn't watched him with the eyes of a woman and yet, to her distress, she had to admit that, unwillingly, the woman inside her had peeked.

That thought formed a line between her eyebrows and that line deepened when the woman realized that she hadn't felt anything from the unknown man. She'd experienced some tension and the peripheral edges of worry but nothing else.

Now, Leah worried. That had happened to her only once in the past, when she'd been confronted with a psychopath during her first years in the police force.

She'd been puzzled at the time as well but then her mother showed her that the explanation was at hand. It was perfectly normal not to sense a thing from a psychopath. They don't experience any kind of emotions, and therefore there are no vibes for Leah to catch.

She'd made her business to know everything about psychopaths at the time and nothing she'd learned encouraged her when it came to dealing with such people.

That was Leah's main concern here. Her inability to reach out to that man's emotions could mean only one thing and that wasn't very encouraging.

"Shouldn't we be going, Leah?" Mark asked. At the same time, his eyes were surveying the garden. He was trying to find out what had upset Leah so much that she'd frowned like that and forgotten about leaving the premises.

Leah glanced at him and barely managed to hide her surprise when she heard his voice. She'd been so lost in her thoughts that she'd forgotten about Mark.

She glanced back in the direction that the man had taken but of course he'd already disappeared. She showed Mark a crooked smile and nodded.

"Yeah, I think we should be going, Mark," she agreed and then started the car.

Leah followed the alley leading to the other end of the garden, her eyes attentive to the curves in the road. Yet, her mind was still on the man that she couldn't read and that had swiftly disappeared before she could see his face.

CHAPTER 3 – DIRTY DISHES IN THE AFTERMATH OF A PARTY

When she got back to the office with Mark in her tow, the detective squad was full of noises and movement as always. Anyway, Leah had learned to ignore the cacophony of sounds. She would surround herself in a bubble of isolation and concentrate on her own conversations or on the research she had to do at a certain moment. She'd stopped noticing what was going on around anymore. It was just background noise.

She was content, in any case, that by then, smoking on the squad floor had been forbidden. She could still remember the smog and smell that always lingered around a few years back at the beginning of her career. Her eyes would turn red and watery for days and sometimes she had bouts of coughing that required a lot of co-ercion to go away. She'd drunk so much raw egg yolk that she was afraid she would start cackling one day.

Working in those conditions had never been too easy. Of course, people had grumbled and protested the new rules but to no avail.

Leah respected other people's rights as much as the next person. However, she expected that her rights to breathe clean air be respected as well.

She hadn't gotten involved in any of the arguments at that time, though. She'd known that the new smoking rules would be in force without her contribution and that was why she kept quiet.

It turned out to be a very wise deci-sion. Leah thought that her reserve was the reason everyone still spoke to her.

Those heated discussions divided people that had been friends for eons. They broke into two fighting camps and many of a friendship dissolved and never mended in the aftermath of the boisterous war.

Anyhow, two years back, Leah quietly snuk into one of the corner offices. That was what she thought at least but in reality, her tenacity and audacity in solving cases had helped her advance in the ranks and affirm her competence in the field.

The rank of lieutenant opened the door of that office, not Leah's ability to talk her way in. The policewoman might have entertained the belief that she was an accomplished diplomat but her empathic abilities didn't give her the necessary skills to grease her way up the ladder.

Not that she had too much tact. There were moments when she was far too direct and liked to give people a piece of her mind. People's memories were long and they never forgot.

Once in her office, Leah signaled Mark, who'd followed her, to close the door behind him. She didn't think of hiding something from the detectives in the squad anyway because the entire wall to the squad was glass. Still, that glass was thick enough and represented a barrier of sorts for the omnipresent clamor. She needed that buffer as she wanted to start on the case without any kind of inconsequential interruptions.

The young woman sat down and turned her computer on. As she knew that the computer liked to take its sweet time to run the initial software, she turned her pad on as well and waved Mark to sit in one of the chairs before her desk and do the same.

Her office was functional. There wasn't an object in there that didn't fulfill a practical function. Leah wasn't too fond of frills when it came to her working space. She'd found out that she preferred them at home where certain people didn't have access and couldn't catch a glimpse into her psyche.

Not even a photo warmed the top of her desk. Only three small baskets she regularly filled with snacks softened the Spartan décor. Leah considered them practical. She didn't always have the time to go out and eat during the day.

"So, Mark, let's see what you have there," she invited him to start the discussion.

Mark nodded but first, he leaned over her desk and checked the little baskets with snacks carefully, just to notice that she had filled them with grapes, cashews and peanuts. Now, that was disappointing and the line between his eyebrows deepened.

The day before she'd had a selection of cookies and he'd enjoyed every one of them. The man scowled with dismay, yet absent mindedly took a grape and popped it into his mouth. Only then he turned his attention to his pad, as well.

Leah smiled amused and turned her eyes to the computer so that he wouldn't be embarrassed. She didn't want him to see that she was monitoring his moves.

She found Mark very entertaining with his childlike tastes. She'd changed the type of snacks on purpose. It was her small and petty revenge because the other day, he wiped every single cookie on her desk. She'd only nibbled on one and swiftly there weren't any left.

Leah knew that she was somewhat mean but she enjoyed his reactions and if she provided the snacks, the least he could do was to provide the entertainment.

"I talked with Mr. Papadopoulos, the owner of the house," Mark began, "and I found out that he'd had a party last night. It didn't end till the wee hours of the morning," he made a point to specify and then, he glanced up at her. Leah nodded and that was his cue to continue. He checked on his pad and said, "I understand that he'd had about sixty guests and he couldn't confirm everyone's whereabouts during the party… Given the number, I think it would have been impossible," he observed, glancing at her again.

"Yeah, it would," she agreed softly, although she imagined that a man of Mr. Papadopoulos's means would have had the necessary personnel to keep track of all those guests.

A man with his status wouldn't have allowed anyone to trespass in certain areas of his house. He would have a sizable number of security people on his payroll to secure boundaries.

Mark nodded, satisfied, and continued his report, completely oblivious to Leah's thoughts, "I understand that the victim, Klavdiya, wasn't on the list."

"How come?" Leah asked and leaned forward.

Her curiosity was piqued. That the victim wasn't on the list didn't sound quite right. No one should have been able to crash a party in the circles where Mr. Papadopoulos moved. Even a beautiful woman like Klavdiya would have encountered resistance.

"I meant that her name wasn't on the list," Mark corrected his statement hastily. "She was under *'plus one'*," he thought to add. Leah was very particular about his being very specific.

"Ah, I see," the woman's understanding shone in her eyes. "She came with someone else."

Mark nodded in agreement and looked back at his pad, "A Mr. Angelus…"

"And where was Mr. Angelus when his date was killed?" she asked in a harsh voice.

"He'd left a couple of hours earlier. I mean a couple of hours before the victim was seen in the house the last time," Mark rushed to add.

He knew that Leah didn't like it when her officers weren't precise in details and he'd already slipped once. It wasn't as if she'd been vicious but her eyes drilled into the offender and no one felt comfortable when Leah went into scolding mode. Even his parents' lectures over the years had seemed more bearable.

"Why? Why did he leave without her?" Leah leaned over the desk once more and braced her elbows on the sides of the keyboard.

"Someone said… it was an assumption actually," Mark thought to point out so that he wouldn't mislead her, "that Mr. Angelus and his date had a discussion. She seemed interested in staying and he was interested in leaving… So, he just left…"

"And the host didn't say anything…" Leah noted pensively.

"He didn't because Mr. Angelus never said *'goodbye'*," Mark thought to mention.

"How come?" Leah perched on the edge of her chair and tilted her head to the right inquiringly.

The etiquette in those circles would have required a few polite words before leaving the host's house.

Mark blushed and looked down. Leah mused because she had a good guess about what he needed to say.

44

She'd heard him pulling a raw one to the boys in the past and he'd never blushed. Or at least, he hadn't blushed before his eyes fell on her.

It looked like her subordinate was concerned about stating some things in her presence as if they'd lived in the Victorian era and he couldn't tarnish her perception of the world.

That was another constant source of amusement for her. It was downright funny albeit a little puzzling for her to see that the thought that she already had a certain perception of the world, which included abominable crimes and far worse things than what he could say in his jokes or reports, never crossed the detective's mind.

Mark was a contradiction in terms. Just a couple of years older than Leah, he either acted like a teenager or like a concerned parent before her and, sometimes, she found it difficult to balance the man's two sides. Sometimes she even had doubts about his mental balance although he seemed normal enough.

"All right, Mark, just spell it out," she cajoled him into spilling the beans. The smile flourishing on her lips didn't lack some malice, though.

"Well… the host was otherwise engaged…" Mark explained evasively.

"With?" she insisted mulishly.

"With… a beautiful model, with skin rivaling alabaster and such long and shapely legs that would have made Venus weep…" the officer continued and then glanced up at her just in time to see her eyebrows going up. He tapped his finger on the pad and specified, "That's what he said, word for word."

"I see," she murmured. "Do we have any picture of this… modern Venus, Mark? We should get an idea for ourselves," she explained to a mortified Mark.

For a moment, the man had feared that she implied that he already had a picture with the fashion model and he couldn't fathom why she'd think that of him. Leah had sensed his outrage and tried to smooth his feathers.

"No, not really…" Mark stuttered somewhat.

His eyes were focused on the geometrical pattern of the carpet as if he'd found something extremely interesting there, something that hadn't been there for the last two months since the carpet was replaced. Then he glanced back to her and proposed, "We can try on the Internet. I'm sure that there must be a photo with her…"

Leah invited him with a wide gesture, "By all means, be my guest, Mark, find one."

With nimble fingers, Mark opened the browser on his pad and started a search with the model's name. The avalanche of pages dedicated to the woman startled him.

"Should we try only images?" he asked Leah. "There are so many pages with mentions of her…" he shook his head, at a loss of words.

"Let's try just images for the moment," she acquiesced. "We'll go through the rest if there's any need later."

The man clicked on images and the page turned to tens of pictures reflecting the cold beauty of a modern Venus. Leah hadn't missed her target. Her label was more than appropriate.

The detectives looked from one photo to another and everywhere they saw the same impersonal and cold smile. White and perfect teeth, an elegant arch of the lips but no sparkle in the eyes. However, they both had to admit that the host of the party was very close in his description. The modern Venus's skin rivaled alabaster and her limbs were supple and beautifully shaped.

"Now, I understand Mr. Papadopoulos," Leah said quietly. "He wouldn't have cared if all his guests had left without a word. Not when he busied himself with… such a delightful creature."

Mark didn't think it was necessary for him to add anything more. His boss had already touched on the heart of the matter.

"So, now we know what the host was doing when his guest met her demise. Do you have the list with the others?" the lieutenant asked the officer.

Mark nodded enthusiastically and showed his pad as a proof, "Yes, we do. Mr. Papadopoulos asked his head of security to provide me with the entire list. The name of everyone invited is here and there's a sign next to each of the people that actually came to the party. There were a few that didn't make it," he specified.

"Interesting," Leah replied softly. "I'd have thought that his parties would be irresistible and no one would miss their chance to attend…"

"I suppose…," Mark agreed reluctantly. "Yet, people get sick or…"

She waived his concern away and replied, "We'll see, no worries, Mark. We have to check all of them…"

"Even the people who didn't attend the party?" he asked in a shocked voice. He glanced at his boss with wide eyes, almost ready to pop out of their sockets.

Sixty people meant a lot of people and he didn't see the reason to question everyone. Not to mention that people who were living in that circle didn't comply easily with police's requests for answers.

"All of them," she repeated stubbornly and then grinned at him. "Imagine, Mark, how many people you'd get to bother. Don't tell me you won't enjoy being on this side of the net, as you'll be the one asking questions," she mocked him.

As a matter of fact, she'd had the occasion in the past to read his overt pleasure whenever he interviewed suspects or witnesses. She'd sensed that he sometimes perversely enjoyed having the control over those people and she didn't like it. She'd been waiting for a good while to catch a chance to rub his nose into that.

"But sixty people…," he mumbled completely oblivious of Leah's objective.

His narrowed eyes and the tension lines gathered on his forehead proved that he was concerned only with the huge load of work, which would fall mostly on his shoulders. Hence, the thought that the lieutenant was simply pushing his buttons never occurred to him.

Leah rolled her eyes at his shortsightedness. It was typical for Mark. That was why she was sitting in the lieutenant chair and not Mark. He was a good officer but couldn't perceive the entire picture.

Leah sighed deeply to keep her disappointment under control. She imagined throwing the pad and nailing Mark directly in the middle of his forehead.

Sometimes his skull turned out to be too thick. He'd completely miss the lessons she tried to teach him. In such moments, she felt the urge to give him a good shake and make him open his eyes.

"Well," Leah shrugged with indifference, "you'll take the first thirty and I'll take the remaining thirty," she said as if it had been the easiest task in the world.

Her lips bowed in a smile when she saw the grimace of displeasure on Mark's face. A tinge of guilt probed the edge of her mind but she muffled it. He deserved it.

"I have plans," he mumbled and his fingers unwittingly began a staccato on the desk top.

"What was that?" she tilted her head and feigned that she hadn't heard him.

"Nothing, nothing," he hastily said. "Maybe we should bring Josh and Anna into this," he said, grasping at straws.

"Oh, I intend to," Leah assured him nonchalantly. "Josh can follow up with Venus here and…"

"Why?" Mark wailed before he could control himself.

Leah's eyebrows raised on top of her forehead as the shock at the man's whimper made her incapable of uttering a syllable.

She eyed him with circumspection. The officer definitely didn't have a good day. He had jumped out of the frying pan into the fire.

"I beg your pardon?" the lieutenant inquired sitting straighter in her chair

She'd expected him to try and convince her to let him handle the model. He was a man after all and no man would have handed over to another man his chance to interact with such a fine specimen of a woman.

Apparently, her expectations were far off. The wail that came from her subordinate was something she'd never heard before.

The emotions coming from him were a total mess. For a few seconds, their force made her incapable of reading anything. His despair, hopelessness and regret enveloped her and she scowled.

Sometimes it wasn't such a good thing that she could feel what others felt. The intensity of Mark's present feelings overwhelmed her and made her palms clammy.

"Mark, look at me," Leah looked directly at him and asked in a flat voice.

She knew that talking without passion was a better way to make him listen to her.

She waited patiently until Mark finally glanced at her and then she continued in the same flat voice, "If you become so volatile when you hear that I'm thinking of assigning another officer to speak to her, it's better that you don't. Your interview with this woman wouldn't be of any use to us and I'm pretty sure that you'd see that as well if you stopped whimpering and started thinking hard... You'd just make an ass of yourself, Mark..."

Leah looked at his bowed head and patted the back of his hand reassuringly. There were times when she had the feeling that men needed more reassurance than their counterparts.

Mark didn't look up and didn't reply. She sensed his mortification and shook her head. A brief smile played on her lips for a few moments.

After a brief moment of reflection, she observed, "I'm afraid that even Josh might not be a good choice for this task... Anna will interview the model," she decided and then, she turned to the desktop and entered her password.

Mark understood that the discussion was over and he was smart enough not to pursue it further. He knew that whenever Leah made a decision, there was no way to dissuade her and he didn't dream of trying.

The lieutenant was easy to work with as long as people didn't step over the boundaries she'd set out. He'd learned that the hard way and didn't care for another lesson.

"Do you want me to send you the guest list? How do you want to divide the names between us?" Mark asked subdued.

The lieutenant's explanation had chastised him enough. He still couldn't believe that he'd reacted like an untried teenager and that before his boss. The officer was afraid that the embarrassment wouldn't go away soon and he had the urge to smack himself over the head for his stupidity. Repeatedly.

"Yes, please, do," she replied absentmindedly and opened the search option in her software. "It might be easier if I took the names directly from the list instead of having you spelling the names for me… Mark, go into the squad room and call Anna and Josh in. They should be there by now," she continued without sparing a glance to Mark.

She pretended to read something very interesting in her office email and didn't take her eyes off the monitor until she noticed that Mark had left the office.

Leah would have loved to be able to block all those embarrassing feelings that came from Mark wave after wave. She felt sorry for the man but some part of her couldn't stop thinking that it was shameful that a thirty-year old man wasn't able to control himself and that his reactions put her in such a bad position in the process.

She resented him because of that although she had to admit to herself that he wasn't aware of what was going on and blaming him was unproductive.

The detective shook her head and pushed those thoughts to the back of her mind. She had other things to do and she turned her focus to the search. She began with Klavdiya's name and in a few seconds, the data populated the screen.

The information about the woman confirmed some of the things she'd already read before the body turned stone cold.

The woman was born in Russia indeed although the name of the locality blinking on the screen didn't say anything to Leah. She'd never been too fond of geography and in school, she studied just enough to graduate, and nothing more.

Curiosity made her open another browser and google the town's name. She found out that indeed the small town was Rostov, an old town situated in Yoroslavy Oblast. It had been erected on the shore of the lake Nero. Huh, that was an interesting name for a lake, she thought, her curiosity in over drive. She made a mental note to check it later. She had other things to verify right then.

Leah had had her mental readings confirmed more than once over the years, yet, the policewoman in her still had doubts and needed to double check every piece of information. She couldn't afford to leave anything to chance when catching a killer hung in the balance.

The detective returned to the data displayed in the police software search and checked the civil status of the woman. Leah learned that indeed the victim was divorced and had one son. She immigrated to Canada when she was very young where she built a steady life for both of them.

She worked for the same company during the entire life she spent in the adoptive country even though she'd enjoyed a very low increase in salary along the years. The figures showed that she'd had only a two percent increase in pay every year and that increase wouldn't have accounted for inflation. That she'd never looked beyond that to find a new job was telling.

When she touched her hand, Leah had sensed that Klavdiya Alekseyeva was a creature of habit. She wouldn't have left the comfort of a cushy job, even though it didn't pay too much. The woman wouldn't have tried to find something better or something more challenging. She might have harbored such notions now and then but she wouldn't have acted upon those feelings because Klavdiya wasn't the type of person who'd challenge the status quo.

The officer didn't find any notable relationships listed in her search and turned to the victim's son. She hoped that she could unearth something helpful in his profile.

Daniel Alekseyev was twenty-one now and appeared to have been a self-sufficient young man for the last three years. He'd been listed at a different address than Kavdiya's ever since he turned eighteen.

So, he wasn't a momma's boy, at least on paper, Leah concluded. Still, she needed to meet him face to face to be sure.

His profile also showed constancy in his work habits. Apparently, Daniel had worked for the same company for the last six years. He'd started out as a part time employee while in high-school and continued with a full-time job afterwards, although he attended college at the same time. His choice in studies showed that he intended to continue working for the same company after graduation.

The young man appeared to have inherited his mother's contentment with respect to his work and didn't entertain any ideas of changing the direction of his career.

At least he'd had more substantial pay increases over the years, Leah observed when she checked the income tab. In some ways, that set him apart from his mother somewhat.

Leah opened the tab listing relationships and noticed that he'd just got married. The young woman who became his wife had shared his dwelling for the last three years.

The wedding, apparently celebrated with all the trimmings, had taken place exactly a month earlier. His mother's death would have marked the one-month anniversary and that piqued Leah's attention.

That wasn't the only reason that made the detective turn her nose to the news of Daniel's marriage. She doubted that someone at that age could discern between lust or infatuation and the real deal.

In her opinion, strong relationships needed time, even a few years to develop and sustain the proof of time, although there were some exceptions to the rule, she admitted. But those were few and far between.

Leah shrugged, unwilling to explore the idea in more depth and returned to her search. She noted Daniel's home and work addresses and phone numbers to contact him that very day.

After a furtive glance at her watch, she decided that she would visit him at work after a couple of hours. He needed to be notified about his mother's demise, after all, and she didn't want him to hear the news from mass media.

Leah changed the parameters of her search to check Klavdiya's employer, Larissa Petrova.

She'd had the time to read only the information under the civil status tab when she heard the door open. She looked up and saw Anna, Mark and Josh gathered in the doorway.

"We knocked at the door, boss, a couple of times but you didn't appear to hear so...," Mark explained their invasion in her personal space and accompanied his words with wide gestures.

Uncertainty rang in his voice and Leah frowned. She disliked his hesitation.

She expected respect but not fear and Mark left the impression that he had his boundaries somehow messed up. Leah didn't have time to set him straight right then so she waved his concerns away and invited them to sit.

As she rarely worked with more than two or three people, she kept the number of seats in the office minimal. She had exactly three chairs.

She'd skipped over the offer of a sofa or anything on those lines. If she needed to sleep, she could go home. When she worked, she didn't need the flat surface of a couch to invite her to slack off in her job.

The officers sat down with their pads in hand and Leah smiled. She'd trained them well. Long gone were the days when one of them would come with their hands in their pockets as if she'd invited them to a friendly chat.

"I've already started on checking the victim and her close connections," she began and glanced from one to the other.

They nodded in unison and her smile widened. She glanced back at her screen and her fingers tapped on the keyboard.

"I've divided the list between us. I think we should go with two teams at all times, or almost at all times," she corrected herself and leaned back in her chair. "Anna, I want you to interview our model, Sybil Miller, alone. I have the feeling that taking Josh with you for this interview would hamper the results," she explained and glance slyly at Josh who grimaced.

She sensed that Mark had already told Josh about the beautiful model and he'd hoped that he would have a chance to be in the same room with her. Josh had seen photos with her before and had hot dreams featuring Sybil many a night.

Leah considered the wisdom of saying something caustic about his hopes and ambitions but decided against opening her mouth on the subject. She'd have had a hard time explaining how she knew about his most intimate desires.

"I divided the remaining of the list in two and already sent your list to your emails," she explained to Anna and Josh. "I need answers, and I need them soon.

Find out who saw the victim, when and with whom. Don't forget, if she went out into the garden with someone, we need that person's name, description and so on," she pointed out and tapped her finger on the desk.

Leah looked from one to the other and then she added, "You know how to do your job. You don't need a refresher course right now," she concluded and noticed with satisfaction that all of them nodded in earnest.

The three detectives stood up and turned to the door when Leah said, "You're with me, Mark."

Mark scowled before he turned to her. He liked working with Leah. Usually. Yet, that day he'd made too many mistakes and he didn't feel comfortable around her. He'd have liked a couple of days to regroup. Anna and Josh left the office and Mark looked after them with longing.

Leah, always leaning back in her chair, observed him with amusement. She knew that he'd liked to have left her office as well.

"All right, Mark. We have to go," she said and locked her computer screen.

She stood up and retrieved her pad off the desk. She also picked up her handbag although she didn't enjoy having to carry it around.

The days were hot now though and wearing a jacket was out of question. Without the large pockets of her jacket, she didn't have anywhere to pile the things she needed. Hence, she had to carry that bag with her everywhere.

Mark opened the door for Leah and followed her into the squad room. People were milling around and the sound of several voices assaulted the two detectives like a shock wave. Leah hurried her step and she didn't stop before reaching her car.

"We'll take my car, Mark. It's more practical," she said and the officer didn't reply although she knew well that he didn't like it when she was driving.

Mark might have had some broad views regarding male and female roles. Yet, driving didn't enter those views. The idea that a woman would chauffeur him around wasn't very palatable to him, and Leah had sensed that frequently. Since she loved driving, she didn't care much about his misogynistic opinions.

CHAPTER 4 – SKELETONS IN THE CLOSET

As directed by the navigational control, Leah parked behind a small building and picked up her things before she got out of the car. The heat wave hit her and stole her breath. The humidity in the air clung onto her skin with clammy fingers. Sweat dripped along the back of her neck and between her breasts.

Mark had already climbed out of the car and was surveying the building, his hands fisted in the pockets of his trousers. He was whistling a merry tune while counting the floors and she resented that the man didn't seem to mind the high temperatures.

The building was almost hidden in a pocket of trees. It wasn't one of the sky-scrapers they would see downtown. Still, the buildings around the area had around seven or even ten floors while that one was low rise. Mark counted four floors, main floor included.

"Kind of isolated," Leah observed, and Mark nodded pensively.

"Probably they don't need visitors here," he replied.

"I don't think they do," she agreed. "I understand that they create and test computer games. I imagine there's a constant market for such products," she added inquiringly.

"You can't even imagine," Mark said. "I have two nephews and they are crazy about this sort of thing. My sister complains all the time about the money she spends on new games."

"Well, they're not for me," Leah shrugged.

She'd never found a reason behind punching away on the keyboard just to evade a dwarf or a dragon or whatever. The computer was a tool for her and she understood to use its potential but she wouldn't care to stare at a screen and play at make believe. Her life was full as it was and she'd always resisted the pressure of her peers and never got involved in futile entertainment.

They climbed the stairs and entered the lobby of the building. Instantly, the cool air inside stole their breath. The difference between the stuffy atmosphere outside and the arctic air inside the building came as a shock to their bodies. Leah shivered and took a squint at Mark. He didn't fare better than she did and that soothed her pride.

At the beginning of her career, she'd been frequently judged because she was a female. She couldn't forget people's biased behavior and double standard. That was why she'd promised herself never to let her gender come into question, even though she was aware that there were some natural differences between men and women. She still tried hard to compensate.

Changes took place all over the police force and women gained more terrain during the last few years. She still had to put up with oblique glances when the crime scene was excessively gruesome or when her temper got the best of her.

She could read in the men's mind the idea that she might fall apart or that she was bitchy because it was that time of the month and hormones obstructed her reasoning.

It was true that sometimes during those periods she lost her patience faster, but hormones didn't account for other times. She was plain angry because someone had screwed up or because someone had chosen not to listen to her orders.

Leah shook the upsetting thoughts away and made a bee line to the front desk where a young woman, almost a teenager, was buttoning on a keyboard with a vengeance. At the same time, she was answering the calls that came through the headset she had perched over her thick purple hair.

Once she reached the reception desk, the detective cleared her throat to make their presence noted. Mark stopped right behind her and his emotions assaulted her. She became aware that the young woman mesmerized him.

The receptionist took her eyes off her monitor for a second and offered them a smile that could have rivaled Sybil's.

Leah didn't need to bother and read Mark's thoughts or feelings to know what he was thinking. His sudden gasp explained everything.

The man was spellbound. The young woman's freshness and beauty surprised and awed him. Leah had to admit jealously that the woman delivered a serious punch to any man who was still alive.

That favorable impression lasted only one second. The woman gestured to them to wait and returned to her keyboard.

Now, it was Leah's turn to be impressed. She couldn't believe the receptionist's gumption. She just glanced at them, smiled and then returned to her game. Leah was sure she was playing a video game considering how she used that keyboard.

"Miss," the detective called out in a sharp voice and had the pleasure to see the young woman's head snap up. "We don't have the time to wait for you to finish that game," she continued harshly.

The receptionist narrowed her eyes but didn't reply. She pushed the keyboard aside and with a cold smile now, she asked, "What can I do for you?"

Leah noticed that her willingness to help had turned as cold as the Arctic, yet she didn't care. She didn't care for the tinges of disappointment that came from Mark either. He wasn't supposed to make conquests during work hours anyway.

"We need to speak to Daniel Alekseyev," the detective replied with clipped words. The sunlight reflected in her green-bluish eyes and highlighted her coldness.

Still, Leah and Mark had to admire the receptionist. She didn't seem impressed with the detective's frigid appearance and kept a businesslike attitude.

She matched Leah's cold demeanor and inquired, "Are you having an appointment?"

The policewoman replied, "No, we aren't. Yet, we don't need one," she added and her smug smirk disconcerted the young woman who seemed baffled for the first time. Leah was positive that no one had ever given her such a reply before.

"How come?" the younger woman retorted with belligerence after only a few seconds of hesitation and her self-confidence earned Leah's respect.

She wouldn't have expected to see such a young individual recover so fast. That girl was something else and Leah made a note to get to know her better if she had the chance. Meanwhile, she dug into her handbag and took out her police ID and badge.

Although the receptionist's sudden curiosity and trepidation were palpable, the only exterior sign of her excitement was a slight dilation in her pupils. She nodded briefly and then she dialed an extension, her eyes always on the two detectives.

"Mr. Alekseyev, the police are here to see you," she said in the most professional tone she could muster and Leah's mouth sketched a smile.

"I understand, sir," the woman replied to something she was told and disconnected the call. She looked at Leah and said, "He'll be downstairs in a couple of minutes. Would you have a seat?" she waved towards the seating area near the far corner of the lobby where the sun played the various colors of the chairs and brightened the floor.

"We'll wait here," Leah responded and leaned onto the front desk bracing herself on an elbow.

She turned her head to the other corner of the lobby where a multitude of potted plants were competing for sunlight. The thought that someone got the things wrong and placed the flowers where the waiting area should have been crossed her mind.

A glance at Mark made her aware that he was trying to make nice with the girl at the front desk but he didn't have too much luck. The young woman had already returned to the game on her monitor and stopped paying attention to them.

Leah mused when she perceived the man's frustration but only for a moment. She reprimanded herself severely.

Lately, she'd been out of sorts somewhat and started taking pleasure in seeing Mark suffer or make mistakes. That wasn't something she should have been comfortable with and she frowned, angry with herself.

She heard the elevator doors open and turned towards the sound just in time to see a casually dressed young man emerge from the elevator. His gait was athletic and showed that the man liked to exercise on a regular basis and keep in shape.

He might have been computer addicted, as his profile implied, yet he still seemed to find time for other things and that spoke of a balanced life regimen.

The lieutenant envied him. She'd never had the ability to balance things. Either she would overdo some or underdo others but she would never get them quite right. She lacked the skill to find the right dose in everything.

Leah also noticed that Daniel Alekseyev took after his mother. The young man had the same white skin set off by disheveled curly black hair. He was looking at her with his mother's hazel and slightly slanted eyes.

Initially, when she saw Klavdiya for the first time, Leah had thought that her negligent hairstyle was the result of long hours of exhausting styling. Now, she wondered if the victim hadn't just been lucky to have been gifted with a willful head of hair which just worked in her favor.

Keeping her eyes on Daniel, she noticed that there were some differences between mother and son, as well. Daniel's chin was square and shadowed by the beginning of a hopeful beard. That detail made him look stronger than Klavdiya. The woman's weak chin didn't recommend her as a strong character in Leah's eyes.

The man's eyes showed concern and worry. Leah knew that she had to tell him what happened and probably shake his world in the process. She didn't enjoy that part of her job but it was hers nonetheless and she took her responsibilities seriously.

Leah, with Mark in tow, walked slowly towards Daniel and extended her hand, "I'm Lieutenant Leah MacKay and this is my colleague, detective Mark Dion."

The man didn't bother to introduce himself. Probably, he thought that they already knew who he was. He shook their hands and a courteous smile fluttered on his lips.

Yet, Leah perceived the tension he tried to hide and she decided not to prolong the unpleasant moment.

"Is there somewhere where we could speak without being interrupted, Mr. Alekseyev?" she asked him with a glance in the direction of the receptionist who conveniently forgot about her game and was eying them with unmasked curiosity.

Daniel tilted his head and seemed to ponder her suggestion for a moment. Then he proposed, "Let's go in one of the meeting rooms on the first floor. No one will disturb us there and it is quiet."

He turned to the woman at the reception and asked her, "Jen, would you verify and see which meeting room is free for the next hour?"

The receptionist replied softly, "Of course, Mr. Alekseyev," and turned to her keyboard. Deftly, she checked the schedule and informed him with a warm smile, "The Willow room is free, sir, for the following couple of hours anyway. Would you like me to reserve it for you?"

"Yes, please, do so. Thank you, Jen," Daniel nodded to her and then he showed them to the elevator.

Leah sensed that he'd have liked to ask questions and tried hard to restrain himself. She also detected that he was somewhat terrified of the answers he'd receive from them. She felt sorry for him but she couldn't alleviate his fears.

After a brief trip in the elevator, Daniel chose to take a right on the corridor. He led them through a maze of cubicles and Leah was convinced that she wouldn't be able to find her way back to the elevator, had he chosen not to show them the way. Even Mark gave signs of confusion and apprehension.

The lively sound of games came from everywhere and all sorts of exclamations enveloped the three people who were advancing across the open floor. Leah's eyebrows shot up at some of the most colored interjections.

"This is one of the testing floors," Daniel explained apologetically. "Don't worry, though, detectives. We won't hear anything from the meeting room. They're soundproof. I mean all meeting rooms are soundproof," he explained further, and Leah could discern the increased tautness in his voice.

It wasn't something they wouldn't encounter on a daily basis when meeting with people the first time. The word '*police*' had that effect on almost everyone. Few kept their composure in such situations.

Both detectives nodded their understanding and continued to follow him closely. None of them wanted to be left behind.

Finally, Daniel Alekseyev stopped in front of a massive door and input a code on the pad mounted on the wall. The door opened with a resonant click and he invited them to enter the room.

Once the door closed behind them, they found themselves in an oasis of tranquility. No sound came from the cubicles shut out beyond that door or from the street that gleamed behind the window panels that covered the entire far wall.

"Nice setting," Mark murmured, and then. glanced quickly at Leah.

Leah guessed that he wanted to check if she'd heard him. He wasn't supposed to be impressed with the layout of the room, but to pay attention to the people involved in the case.

She chose to let it pass though. It seemed quite petty to reproach him such a slight error. It wasn't like she hadn't had enough opportunities to pick on him if she wished.

Daniel invited them to sit in the armchairs framing a conference table. Leah chose a chair across from Daniel and allowed herself a moment to enjoy the feel of the plushy armchairs.

All the way there, she'd feared that she would have to sit in a leather chair and she hated those types of chair in summer, even if there was air-conditioning in the room. They made her think of sweat and she doubted they were hygienic enough. In theory, the cleaning staff should have cleaned them every day, but somehow she doubted they did it.

After they sat down, Daniel looked from a detective to the other and finally found the courage to ask, "What happened?"

His eyes showed genuine distress and Leah sympathized with him. The waves coming from him revealed that he wondered if something was wrong with his wife and she decided to let him know everything at once. She didn't believe in tormenting someone without a good cause.

She knew it wouldn't be easy for him to hear what she had to say. She leaned on the table and braced herself on her elbows.

In her best soothing voice, Leah said, "I'm very sorry, Mr. Alekseyev, but I have to inform you that your mother passed away."

Daniel's distressed gasp filled the quietness of the room. Both Leah and Mark were watching him closely, although they doubted he had anything to do with his mother's murder.

The way she died had been cruel in the extreme. The woman's body was marred with bruises and cuts everywhere, as if a madman had been at work.

The police officers didn't have any reasons to believe that something so serious had happened between mother and son that could have led to such atrocity.

Leah noted that Daniel was fighting back tears and gave him a few more moments to compose himself and to come to terms with the news. It wasn't every day that someone heard such words and was never easy to come to terms with the death of a loved one.

She saw him unconsciously flex his fists on the smooth surface of the conference table. His eyelashes blinked spasmodically and for a moment she did fear he would start crying.

While she understood why he'd do that, she was afraid that she wouldn't know how to calm him and make him answer her questions afterwards.

That was one of the things she always dreaded in such interviews and Mark was of no help there whatsoever. The maximum extent of his help was to pat someone on the back once or twice and even that without too much conviction.

Finally, Daniel composed himself and looked straight into her eyes when he asked in a gruff voice, "What happened? Was she run over or..."

Leah was about to shake her head when she saw Mark do that and she controlled herself. She chose to reply quietly, "No, Mr. Alekseyev. She was murdered last night."

Her words startled him. His eyes widen in shock and his teeth bit into his upper lip. His fingers grabbed the edge of the table with such force that his knuckles turned white.

The extent of distress vibes coming from him made Leah fear that the shock would overwhelm him and he wouldn't be able to help them with anything.

She looked around searching for a solution frantically when she noticed the water cooler in the corner of the room. She nudged Mark discretely.

"Bring him a glass of water," she whispered to him and Mark glanced at Daniel with blank eyes.

Mark needed about a few seconds to understand the lieutenant's request and her reasons. Only then he went to the cooler and filled a glass with water. He brought it back to the table and handed it to Daniel who thanked him in a hushed voice.

The man drank the water in one gulp and then he turned his misty eyes to Leah.

"Who killed my mother?" he asked and Leah noted with satisfaction that his voice sounded stronger. The man had pulled himself together and now they might get somewhere.

"That's what we're trying to find out," she replied and her eyes remained steady on Daniel.

As if he'd felt some kind of blame in her words, he straightened up. "I didn't kill my mother, detective," he retorted in a cold voice and his Russian accent, which had been barely perceptible when the detectives made his acquaintance, became heavier. "I hope you do have other suspects besides me," he added sharply and the implication of his words was clear.

Leah perceived a hint of sarcasm in the man's voice and wasn't sure how to take it.

"Right now, everyone is a suspect," she replied always calm. "I know that the law says that everyone is innocent until proven guilty, but I have to shift the wheat from the chaff and that's not such an easy task."

Her words seemed to have enough impact on Daniel because he nodded his agreement. "What now?" he asked.

"Now, I will ask you about your relationship with your mother," the detective replied and leaned back in her armchair and laid her hands in her lap as if she'd been getting ready to hear a bedtime story.

Daniel took a few moments to answer and then he began, his eyes fixed on a point in a distance, "We used to have a good relationship… Always… She wasn't a very strict mother and her rules were easy to follow… She always encouraged me to be independent, responsible…," he reminisced.

"Yet, something happened," Leah intervened.

The man looked at her and nodded hesitantly. He seemed somewhat reluctant to explain, but her dogged expression gave no quarter.

"I met my wife in high-school… Ninth grade… She wasn't Russian…"

"Was that a problem for your mother?" Mark asked but Daniel shook his head.

"No, she wasn't interested in that. She accepted that Biskane[1] was part of the First Nations. She didn't have any qualms over

---

[1] Biskane – Burning fire – traditional name for First Nations (Anishinaabe)

that. She liked her just fine..." he reaffirmed and then he paused.

Leah saw that he struggled with something and nudged him gently, "If you have something to say, you'd better say it... We'll find out anyway..."

"Oh, it's not that," he waved her concern away. "I was just thinking... I don't want you to judge my mother too harsh but... I suppose there's no other way," he continued and rubbed the root of his nose with his thumb and forefinger.

Leah felt Mark's eyes on her and turned to him. He looked like a man wanting to say something but she stopped him with a slight shake of her head.

She needed Daniel to continue his ideas at his own pace. Along the time, she found out that sometimes interrupting someone's thoughts didn't necessary bring light in a specific matter.

"Appearances played an important role in my mother's perceptions," he said firmly, glancing from one detective to the other. "If a woman was beautiful, my mother would consider her worthy... It didn't matter if that woman was stupid or greedy or... whatever," he clarified and shrugged his shoulders. "My wife, Biskane, is very beautiful," he stated very matter of fact. "When I laid my eyes on her for the first time, she took my breath away," he confessed with a whimsical smile and gesticulated with both hands.

Leah sensed that he felt a little embarrassed but she started to like the man. He seemed real and grounded enough, which was astounding for such a young fellow.

"My mother simply beamed when I brought Biskane at home and introduced her. She was proud that people would see me hand in hand with such a beautiful girl… We were in the ninth grade as I said before…" he tried to gather his thoughts and focused on the wall behind Leah for a few moments.

"My wife is not very tall, detectives," he felt compelled to say, "but she's been blessed with a perfect body and that from early adolescence. Round where it was meant to be round, narrow waist, long legs… Her hair is ink-black, long and shiny. Her cheekbones are high and slightly wide. She is very easy going and in general, she has a happy disposition… It takes a lot to anger her or to see her sad… At the time, I didn't need anything more, of course," he confessed, his thoughts far away. "I was just a teenager controlled by hormones…"

He kept silent for more than a minute but Leah didn't want to interrupt his process of reasoning. Exactly when she became afraid that Mark might intervene, Daniel turned back to them and continued with his story, "After a while, I also noticed that she was smart and kind... I saw that she worked hard… It became evident to me that she wanted to do something with her life – her parents were poor, you see, and her people had been through rough times… I imagine everyone knows that... But she was determined and… And that is something I appreciate in people… And I appreciated the same thing in my mother as well, although I knew that she was frivolous and stuck on appearances most of the time…"

When Daniel stopped again and closed his eyes, Leah understood that he needed some time to recollect. She glanced at Mark and almost smiled when she saw that he was riveted on the story and couldn't take his eyes from Daniel.

Daniel licked his dry lips and Mark immediately jumped out of the chair and brought him another glass of water without needing to be prompted. The man thanked him profusely and then drank every drop of water before he started talking again.

"I moved in with Biskane when I turned eighteen. I'd been working for three years already and even though I started with a few hours part-time, my boss saw some potential in me and gave me more and then more... He pushed me to go to the Toronto Film School and study video game design and animation. He paid for my school, which spared me from taking loans and I was also able to save money from what he paid, and he paid well. When I turned eighteen, I already had a few thousands in savings and investments. He kept promoting me and in not even six years, I'm leader to a design team and I make more than my mother did after almost twenty years... Anyways, after Biskane and I moved together, she started making plans to continue her education, as well. She wanted to become a paralegal and she found out that she could get a loan from OSAP for that. However, I knew that I would marry her one day. I'd known that for a few years already and I didn't want her to be overwhelmed by debt once she finished school so I paid for her tuition. That made sense to me but that was what set my mom up. She was angry and accused... she was very mean to Biskane... She told me that her parents should pay for her school... I pointed out that she didn't pay for mine and that Biskane and I were living together... She fought back dirty... She said that Biskane lived with me only because I made more money than she did and... to be honest, I didn't like it... I told her to get lost... I loved my mother, detectives, but she'd become vicious and unrelenting at the time and... I thought that... if that was what she thought about me and about the woman I wanted to marry... I didn't see the point to waste my time talking to her...," he concluded and looked down at the table top.

Leah saw the lines formed at the corners of his mouth and understood that the man controlled himself only because of his sheer will.

She glanced at Mark and almost burst out laughing. He was so caught in the story that he didn't even blink. He looked like a baby owl and maybe that was the first time that she'd felt something close to tenderness for him.

"That happened three years ago, I understand," Leah told Daniel when the silence stretched too long and he nodded.

"Have you two been at odds ever since?"

"No," he shook his head. "We didn't talk for a few months but got back to normal afterwards… Well, almost normal. There was a strain in our interactions and I knew that it would always be there… I suppose I couldn't forget what she'd said and she couldn't forgive me because I'd cast her away… Ironic enough," Daniel mused, "Biskane and my mother have been the best friends ever since we made up. The strain was just between the two of us…"

"And that was the extent of the dissension between the two of you?" the lieutenant asked and, at the same time, she leaned forward and opened her handbag quietly.

She took her iPad out and put it on the table.

Daniel hesitated a moment but then he decided to be as open as possible. He shook his head and said, "No, it wasn't… As I said, detective, my mother was somewhat trapped in appearances. When I turned sixteen, she decided that her time had just come and that she needed someone. So, she looked around. I didn't say anything at the time because I didn't think it was my place, but she was looking only at men that showed a good front. You know the type, good clothes, stylish haircut, appearance of means…"

Both Leah and Mark approved. They'd seen that type, both female and male, and not only once in their line of work.

"She found one and he moved with us quite fast, in my opinion. It was a matter of a couple of weeks… Then, we understood why. The man owned a few suits and a lot of arrogance. Nothing more. He'd just been fired, although he dressed that up. He explained that he intended to start his own business and that was why he'd left his previous employer. While mother could be infatuated with a good-looking man who knew how to dress, she wasn't willing to pay for his expenses. She intended to find someone who would pay for hers. So, that relationship died fast enough. Within other two weeks he was out of the house and I didn't have to say a thing to move the things along."

"Were there bad feelings on his side?" Leah asked.

"Somewhat, yes, I think," Daniel said reluctantly. "For about a year afterwards, we would have the occasional phone call, especially if the guy drank something before. He would shout and swear. In the end, my mother changed the phone number and the calls ended."

"I think I'd like his full name," Leah observed and turned on her iPad.

"I think his name was Iuri Grigoriev," he answered pensively. "Yes, that was… Russian, of course… For a while we were afraid he was involved with Russian mafia… You know, with all the movies and the press…," he gestured and a sad smile appeared on his lips.

Both Leah and Mark smiled back. Sometimes, imagination got the best in people. Yet, they had to check that Iuri and Leah made a note in her iPad.

"Did she give up finding someone?" Mark intervened.

"No, she didn't, but she didn't find a suitable man until about a year ago… Maybe a little more… Or that was what she thought at the time. This one matched her requirements to the '*t*', with one exception," Daniel explained and rubbed his hands, a sign of anguish in Leah's book.

"What was the exception?" Mark asked again.

"He had a good job and had inherited a lot of money. He was a snap dresser. Yet, he was very stingy. When they moved together, my mother expected him to pay for everything and pamper her. That didn't happen. She had to cajole every cent out of his pocket. Still, she hoped he would marry her and then she would have access to his money…"

Daniel stood up and went to the cooler and poured himself another glass of water. He drank it there, right next to the cooler and after he sipped the last drop, he quashed the plastic cup in his fist and threw it into the bin next to the cooler. He seemed to hesitate a moment and smoothed his hair slowly to buy some time.

Leah sensed that he didn't feel comfortable with the part that followed and that was why she allowed him to take his time and find the most appropriate words. She didn't see that she would gain anything by rushing him.

The man had been open enough and she read him like an open book. He was very straightforward, although he had some remorse now and then whenever he revealed unpleasant things about his mother.

Daniel returned to the table with heavy steps and sat down. That agile gait of his was long forgotten.

He rubbed his hands together and then looked directly into the lieutenant's eyes and said, "I want you to understand and not judge my mother harshly… Believe me, she doesn't deserve it. If circumstances had been different…," he shrugged helplessly.

He reflected with his eyes on the wall behind Leah and then continued, "I want you to have a clear picture, detectives. My

father swept her off her feet in a whirlwind courtship during the summer when
she graduated from high-school. Before
that time, my grandparents had restricted
her outings severely and she hadn't been
allowed to have a boyfriend… She knew
nothing of the outside world… She was
like a ripe fruit ready to pluck… My father
did the plucking," he observed and grimaced with dismay. "They were married
in less than a month, despite my grandparents' opposition. My mother was extremely passionate and dramatic about
her love and she wouldn't be deterred…
They had to relent and let her marry because they were afraid that she would
harm herself. Anyway, she was already at
age and they couldn't do much… My parents lived together for about five years until she found out he had been cheating on
her with every single woman in their circle. He'd slept with her best friends and
even with two of her cousins… And the
cheating part had started right after the '*I
dos*' were spoken… You can imagine that
she was… devastated… The cheating was
bad enough, you see," he said and gesticulated widely, a sign of his agitation.

"Worse was how she found out… They were having a party… My mother had worked hard in the kitchen and on decorations… She had wanted him to be proud of her… One of the women got drunk, very drunk. Almost out of her mind… Too much vodka, I suppose… She was mad at my father. He'd just replaced her with a new conquest and she revealed everything in front of everybody and pointed her finger to all the women present at the party and who'd slept with my father… My mother was livid. She was ashamed and hurt and humiliated. She asked my father to leave that very evening… Actually she asked him after a huge show with lots of broken dishes, yelling and name-calling, head-bashing and hair-pulling… It was a big bash as there were many people involved… Women that passed through my father's bed… Men that found out that they'd been cuckolded… They had about thirty guests, I think. Anyway, the neighbors called the police to settle things down… All their friends abandoned her afterwards… Although I don't know if she could call those people friends… Anyway, he got the friends in the divorce, but she took her revenge. She asked for every single piece of common property and managed to get everything. She didn't leave a spoon behind."

"That's what your mother told you?" Mark asked curious. He knew that divorced parents never told the entire truth.

"No," Daniel shook his head. "I heard a few things at the time. They registered in my mind even though I didn't understand them. I asked my grandmother and she told me everything. Her story was darker than what I've just told you but it's understandable, I think… Of course, later on, I confronted my father during one of the vacations I spent back home, and he confessed… he was older and more mature at the time, although he still found it appropriate to cheat on his new wife…," Daniel shook his head in incomprehension. "Anyway, my point is that my mother worked hard to raise me… She was a good mother… A very good mother… She understood me, taught me to take care of myself, boosted my ambition… Actually, I'm here today because she pushed me to do something with my life… But she was alone. For almost two decades… Not easy for a young woman... Now she wanted companionship, someone who would care for her..."

"And that man you were talking about, didn't offer that to your mother?"

"From what I heard – my mother confessed a lot of things to Biskane, you see, he offered some companionship and was a good lover," Daniel said and blushed.

Leah imagined that it wasn't easy for a man to talk about his mother in that specific context.

"Yet, he cared only about himself and his money. If she'd pushed and made him go shopping with her, she'd have found herself in the situation of paying for everything at the cash register. He would say that he didn't need more than a tomato that evening, for instance. Once, he took her to a restaurant... I remember that she called me excited. She thought he'd changed...," he said and a painful smile flourished on his lips. "At the end of the meal he asked the waiter to bring two bills at the table and instructed her to pay for her dinner... She avoided going out to a restaurant with him afterwards... And they were living together, in her house, for which she paid the rent and all the other expenses…" he explained bitterly.

Yes, Leah thought, that guy sounded like an angel. Just the kind of man to bring home and introduce to your mamma and plan a huge wedding with.

"Anyways, she was alone and he provided some companionship," he concluded. "He didn't mind her shouting and reproaches… He even introduced her to his family and his mother, father and three sisters seemed to adore her… Sometimes she thought that they pushed so much for the continuation of that relationship because George, that was his name, George Alder, didn't have a good track with his relationships. He'd been married for half a year when he was young and all his love affairs lasted less than a month…"

Daniel stopped and looked down at his hands. The silence stretched and the tension in the room itched on Leah's skin.

It touched all of them but Mark was the first to break the quietness, "And what happened next?"

Daniel glanced at him, shrugged and only then replied, "They were together for several months. She was involved in all the Alders' gatherings… That was how everything started, in fact…," he added pensively.

"What started?" Mark inquired again.

"She attended a few picnics, parties, Christmas… You name it… She began to have feelings for George's elder sister's spouse… He courted her secretly… They would meet for a chat in a coffee shop or for a walk in a park. Of course, he skillfully avoided the places where they would meet an acquaintance… He would tell her how unhappy he was and how domineering Lydia turned out to be. She had the control of the money – well, it was hers, so…," Daniel gesticulated to drive his point home.

Mark nodded his agreement and Leah grinned.

Daniel resumed his story, "Anyways, after a while, he came forward and told her that he'd decided to leave Lydia, George's sister, because he loved my mother and couldn't live without her… By that time, mom had thoroughly fallen in love. He lacked money and she didn't care. She believed that their paychecks would make a good living for both of them… That was… astonishing to say the least. I'd never thought I would hear my mother say something like that, detectives…," he shook his head.

He still couldn't believe that radical change in his mother's opinions.

"Anyway, she believed him when he said that he wanted to be with her, and she went straight home and asked George to leave. She told him that their relationship ended."

"How did George take the separation?" Leah asked beating Mark to the punch line. She had the satisfaction to see his mouth tighten in a line.

"Not very well, at first," Daniel admitted. "He didn't believe her and refused to budge. I understand that he merely sprawled on the sofa and started watching TV. Mother got ballistic… She had a temper if someone got on her nerves… She stormed into the bedroom and within half an hour she had all his things packed in bags. She dragged everything outside the apartment and left the bags in the hall of the building. All the while, George watched her with wide and incredulous eyes. Then, he started shouting and pleading, but she wouldn't budge... She told Biskane that she'd finally fallen in love again. It took her over twenty years but she did... She was so infatuated that she didn't even stop to consider the consequences of her decisions...," Daniel shook his head in disbelief.

Leah could feel that his mother's behavior still shocked him and she deduced that there must have been something more to the story.

"It didn't stop there, did it?" she inquired.

"No, it didn't," the man admitted in a tired voice. He rubbed his forehead and continued, "Gareth, that's the guy's name, started visiting mom. He would bring flowers and small gifts. He would take her shopping..."

Daniel stopped and shook his head again. He closed his eyes for a few seconds, and then, he trained his eyes on Leah. His eyes seemed suddenly older and tired.

"He bought her everything she wanted. Yet, for that, he used Lydia's money. He didn't have too much on his

own name. He had a job, but that was all…
He kept saying that he would leave Lydia,
but something intervened all the time.
Mom knew that Lydia was bipolar and
went off the tangent if things didn't happen the way she wanted, and in a way, she
understood Gareth's reluctance in telling
her the truth. At the same time, she
wanted him with her… Biskane tried to
reason with mother and asked her what
would happen if Gareth indeed left Lydia
because he wouldn't have the same financial means. That would mean that all the
gifts and the shopping and their outings
would cease… Mother didn't care. He was
like a poison for her, and I couldn't stop
thinking that it wasn't moral. She was doing to that woman what others had done
to her… And that woman was close to a
sister-in-law somehow," he concluded
and took a break. He stared at the far wall
and licked his cracked and dry lips.

"Would you like some more water,
sir?" Mark asked solicitously.

"Yes, thank you," Daniel replied and
rubbed his face with his palms.

Mark returned to the table with another paper cup full with water and

handed it to Daniel. The man had scarcely sipped from the cup when his cell phone, which she kept in his pocket, rang. He took it out and glanced at the name on the screen.

"It's my wife," he told the detectives. "May I answer?"

"Yes, of course," Leah approved with a wave of her hand.

"Hey, sweetie," Daniel said and his voice sounded very tired in Leah's ears.

She wondered what Biskane thought of that.

"I think we could meet for lunch then, yes," he responded to something his wife said. "All right, then. See you in an hour," he ended the conversation and then glanced at Leah. "I know I reacted presumptuously, but I don't think we need more than an hour to finish this discussion," he said gesticulating suddenly unsure of himself.

"Probably not," Leah admitted. "What happened next?"

"Well, my mother started saying that she couldn't live without him, which she maintained even two days ago... She would have days when she couldn't think

of anyone or anything else but Gareth…
Gareth kept promising he would tell the
truth to Lydia and move in with mom. It
never happened… Though Lydia found
out. How, I don't know, but a month ago
she came to my mother's building and put
on a… let's say, interesting show. No one
will forget her soon, I guarantee. The police were called… She attacked the front
desk guy… She repeatedly clobbered him
over the head with her handbag… I heard
that she had so many things inside that
bag that it felt like bricks… And then she
waited for my mother… Mom hadn't
come from work yet… When she arrived,
Lydia screeched like a lunatic and hit my
mother, as well. She tried to scratch her
eyes out… She called her names… She
even warned her to stay away from her
spouse… You know, it's ironic. Gareth
had already told my mother that he had to
move on and that he couldn't be with her.
He'd decided to go back to Lydia exactly
that morning. … Biskane and I expected
that…He wasn't the type of man who
could live without Lydia's money…. She
pampered him… The woman would have

bought the moon in the sky for him if he'd wanted to."

"Was that the end of the affair?" Leah asked.

"Yes, it was, as far as I know… I know she pinned on him and had days when she couldn't get out of bed… We worried because she showed signs of deep depression… Suddenly, two days ago she told Biskane that she would go to a party with a guy she'd met at the beginning of the week. My wife implored her to be careful because mom didn't know too much about the man. They'd seen each other only twice before his invitation but mom shushed her concerns and assured her that everything would be fine. She said… something on the lines that her life was back on track again…"

"Did you hear anything from her yesterday?" Mark asked.

He shook his head. "We celebrated our one-month anniversary this weekend. We left for Niagara Falls on Friday and returned early this morning. None of us was in contact with anyone before this morning… It was something we decided some time ago… At least once a month to take the time to be just the two of us…," he explained with a nostalgic smile and the detectives smiled back.

The idea of spending some time in isolation in order to reconnect seemed perfect to Leah. She began to reconsider her initial opinion about the couple's marriage.

"Well," she said, "if you give us Gareth's name as well, we can leave you alone," she concluded.

She noted the name down, next to Lydia's and gathered her things. Mark stood up and started towards the door. When he put his hand on the door handle, he frowned and turned back.

"Would you show us the way to the elevator, Mr. Alekseyev?" he asked while Leah pretended to look for something in her bag. She didn't want him to see her grin.

"Of course," Daniel rushed forward and opened the door for them. "It is the company's policy, anyway," he smiled at them but his smile didn't reach his eyes. "No visitors are allowed on the floors without an employee in tow."

"They would get lost probably," Mark mumbled and Daniel glanced at him.

"I think you're right," he replied but didn't continue on that line.

He led the way to the elevator and once he pushed the ground floor button, he asked, "When can I see my mother?"

"Whenever you want," Leah replied softly and touched his arm. "Although, maybe it's better if you called beforehand," she added. "You understand that we have to do an autopsy," she tried to ease him to the idea.

Daniel glanced away but replied in a harsh voice, "I understand, detective, and I support anything that's necessary to catch my mother's killer."

CHAPTER 5 – COFFEE, COOKIES AND AN AUTOPSY REPORT

That morning, Leah opened the door to her office in a huff and threw her blasted handbag on the desk with dismay. God, she hated plodding around with that bag but she couldn't do without.

The small pockets of her cotton pants wouldn't hold many things and the heat wave which stubbornly baked Toronto for the third day in a row didn't allow her to wear anything but a flimsy blouse and cotton pants. Wearing a jacket was out of question.

She plopped into her chair and turned her computer on. She rubbed her eyes to dislodge the sand that grazed her eyeballs. Her morning cold shower had done little to wipe the cobwebs from her eyes and brain.

She knew that she was testy that morning but she couldn't help it. Three days had already passed since they found the victim and they'd put in a lot of overtime. And yet, she didn't have any positive results to show for all the efforts they'd made so far.

Leah pulled up the coroner's report on the screen and started to read it again. She had enough time to review it once more as her team wasn't there yet. They weren't supposed to come until eight and she had forty-five minutes until then.

The coroner had turned the autopsy report in the day before, and Leah's mind was still baffled by what she'd read. Besides, she was very dissatisfied with herself and her empathic perceptions.

It would have been easier if she had found out the name of the killer when she touched a corpse but it didn't work that way. She would catch only a glimpse of the victim's more persistent thoughts and feelings. She would read the vibes that defined that person, but nothing more. Only rarely could she sense something more.

Maybe if she'd refined her gift, she would have been able to sense more, she thought bitterly, her lips pursed. A frown formed between her eyebrows.

Absent-mindedly, she snatched a cookie from one of the baskets she'd restocked the day before. She munched on it and reflected that anyway, she'd been too intent on leaving her family's legacy behind and that was why she hadn't thought clearly at the time.

When she finally realized that her gift would help her even in the profession she'd chosen, it was too late. She didn't have the time to undergo all the training and conditioning she'd been supposed to do when she was younger.

Worse yet, this time around, she hadn't even succeeded to catch important things, she admonished herself with annoyance while she skimmed through the report. Like the fact that Klavdiya had been three-months pregnant at the time of the murder or that the police should look for at least three men.

The DNA tests revealed that three men had been at the scene, although the profiles were not complete. The three men had left behind minute traces of their genetic code but, at least, they did leave something. If they found them, they'd have some forensic evidence to nail them.

The victim had been raped repeatedly and yet the coroner couldn't find any semen inside her. The men hadn't had the courtesy to leave their genetic material behind, she grimaced with disgust.

Leah didn't like the killers that thought ahead and made her job more difficult. She had a strong animosity towards the ones she had to apprehend now. Their brutality had shocked even the coroner's assistant.

The traces that the technicians managed to analyze came from the skin retrieved from underneath Klavdiya's nails and from the residual trace of saliva recovered from one of the bites on her right breast. The culprit had taken care to wipe his saliva afterwards, but his teeth had burrowed deep enough into the skin and some traces of saliva remained lodged inside the wound.

Besides the DNA traces proving the presences of at least three males at the crime scene, the doctor also indicated that three blades had been involved in the systematic stabbing of the victim.

He'd analyzed the depth and shape of the wounds, as well as the angles at which the blades had penetrated the body and proved that three different types of knives contributed to the mosaic of cuts scattered all over Klavdiya's body. He even provided some sketches in case that the police officers had the opportunity to seize the knives.

The depth of the stabbings also showed different strengths, as well as some hesitation in inflicting the wound in some cases. The doctor's report explained how he had reached the conclusion that one of the attackers was left-handed and definitely reluctant to inflict pain.

Perusing the report, Leah appreciated again that the coroner's report was succinct and to the point. Leah had expected as much from Dr. Connelly. He never strayed from the facts and rarely offered any kind of suggestions.

The coroner preferred the cold and precise narrative of science and didn't think it was his place to tell the police officers what to do. That was always a nice change from the other coroners.

Satisfied that she hadn't forgotten any details, Leah closed the file and opened the list with Mr. Papadopoulos' guests, but then she glanced at her watch and saw that it was 7:30. Now she could find some coffee in the squad kitchenette.

Nimbly she stood up and snatched her cup off the desk. She rushed out the door and hurried to the kitchenette.

Sure enough, Nadine, the cleaning lady, had already started making a pot of coffee. She wasn't anywhere in sight but the smell of the Colombian coffee filled Leah's nostrils and her step became livelier.

She camped next to the coffee maker and waited for the last drop to drip into the carafe. At the same time, her foot tapped on the floor and her fingers drummed the rim of the cup.

Her mornings were coffee-fueled and her neuropaths needed their periodical charge of caffeine if she wanted to get results.

The brown liquid seemed to drip forever. Leah tapped her foot some more, whistled a merry tune, and even counted the chocolate bars lined on one of the officers' desk, which she could see through the glass panel of the kitchenette. For a tiny second, she thought of going and grabbing a chocolate bar, but her common sense prevailed.

Through the chocolate-hazed cloud which fogged her mind, she heard the hiss announcing the end of the coffee-making cycle.

That beloved sound almost brought tears in her eyes. Leah was a big girl though and had some self-restraint. She was content to fill her cup to the rim and turned back to her office. Now her step was subdued because she kept taking a sip now and then from the hot liquid.

The list with Mr. Papadopoulos' guests was always on the screen and she dropped into the chair with a groan.

They'd sifted through the people on that damn list for hours and they still had a few more to investigate.

Until then they hadn't uncovered anything useful and their investigation advanced at a snail's pace. They'd encountered lots of faces and haughty glances but nothing to steer them in the right direction.

The only thing that shed some light on the case was the vague description of the man who had led Klavdiya into the garden.

Two matrons had seen them leaving together but they hadn't recognized him. They said that he definitely wasn't from their circle. They described him but their description was sketchy at best. It could have been any tall well-dressed man with a bulky frame. The officers asked the others if they were acquainted with a man corresponding to that portrayal but no one seemed to be sure.

Leah helped herself to another cookie and sipped from her coffee pensively. She was positive that they hadn't encountered any of the suspects.

She might not have been as expert in reading the people as her mother for instance, still she'd have caught a vibe to put her on the right track. She hadn't sensed anything like that.

She nibbled on her cookie and started on a new list. There were only ten people left on the original list and she put five down for Anna and Josh and the others for Mark and herself. She kept on her list the two that hadn't gone to the party and hadn't even bothered to excuse themselves from their host.

CHAPTER 6 – AXEL IS CAUGHT IN THE LINE OF FIRE

Leah balanced her bag on her shoulder and muttered under her breath. She wiped the sweat off her forehead and glanced at the sky. Still no cloud, damn it.

Everybody had been praying for rain for some time now but the weather didn't give any sign of cooperation. One step out of the car and her skin would feel sticky.

Her blouse stuck to her back and she made efforts to ignore it. Gingerly, she crossed the street towards the coffee shop where she'd sent Mark earlier to order coffee and a light lunch for them while she ran across the street to leave a small gift for her mother. It was her mother's birthday the following day and she didn't know if she would have the time for a quick visit.

Leah attempted to push back the thought that she didn't feel like seeing her mother right then but obstinately it kept coming back and bothering her.

Fed up with her parents' constant nagging about her age and life's opportunities passing her by, she grasped at straws when it came to visiting them. Any kind of pretext worked for her.

Anyway, her exhaustion and bad mood didn't go hand in hand with an evening in their company. Sparks were bound to ignite and she had enough tension in her life right then.

Luck had smiled on the lieutenant. The receptionist had informed her that her mother still had twenty minutes left from her counselling session with a patient and invited her to wait.

Leah had seized the opportunity. She'd declined the invitation and hastily, left the gift at the front desk. She'd asked the woman to present her apologies to her mother.

Faced with the baffled expression of the receptionist, she'd explained that she couldn't stay as she was on duty. She hadn't given her a chance to reply and she'd left the office as fast as she could.

She opened the door to the coffee shop and the cool air inside caressed her heated skin. She breathed deeply. Now, that was a nice change after the stuffy air clinging on people outside and her lungs danced with bliss.

Leah looked around and noticed that Mark had commandeered a corner table where no one would disturb them. She mutely gave him the thumbs up and went to join him.

Mark was woolgathering when she reached the table and he didn't see her. She mischievously waved her hand before his eyes and startled him.

A faint blush powdered the man's cheeks and neck and he sprang to his feet. Leah grinned at him and gestured for him to sit down.

"So, what will I have for lunch?" she asked him merrily and that prompted him to watch her with circumspection.

A merry Leah was a contradiction in terms, especially when she was obsessed with a case and she didn't have a solution.

And right then, that was the case and, unfortunately, his reality.

He handed her the sandwich he'd bought and said, "It's salmon. That's what you usually order…"

"Awesome, Mark," she interrupted his explanation with exuberance. "Is this my coffee?" she inquired pointing to one of the cups on the table.

"Yes…," he hesitated waiting for the other shoe to drop. He didn't trust her when she acted so out of character. Leah was stingy with her praises. "Black, no sugar," he thought to add.

Leah thanked him and sipped from her cup, her eyes closing with pleasure. Then she unwrapped her sandwich and inquired, "Have you already eaten?"

Mark nodded. He'd been starving when he got to the shop so he'd already gulped down an entire sandwich in under two minutes. He had to admit that that was a record even for him.

He'd been so famished that he hadn't even thought to wait for Leah. He excused his attitude though. After all, she was the one who'd pushed their lunch break so late.

Leah shrugged and bit daintily into her sandwich. Chewing quietly, she glanced around. The lunch crowd had already disappeared and the noise in the shop had dropped a few decibels.

It worked for her. They still had work to do and they could start discussing the next step right there in the coffee shop.

"So," she said between chews, "we have only one name left on our list and then we have to take a closer look at those Alders and that Grigoriev."

Mark started nodding his agreement, but then stopped. "Grigoriev's dead," he thought to inform her.

Leah sat straighter, wiped her mouth with a napkin and asked, "How do you know that?"

Mark fidgeted in his chair under her inquisitive look but mumbled, "I checked him out."

"Good…What made you do that? Usually I have to push you hard to do something. It's not like you to take the initiative," she observed and thought that probably that was the reason that she'd been promoted before him. The man had a couple of years more than her in the force and logically he should have been promoted.

"That mafia thing," he replied his eyes steady on the table. He didn't feel like facing Leah's sarcasm.

A smile lit Leah's face. That made sense, at least. That mafia reference must have piqued his curiosity and Mark couldn't resist something like that.

"All right, Mark, well done," she shocked him with her words as her praises were few and far between. "How did he die?" she asked.

Mark didn't react to her question immediately. Her approval had caught him unaware and he was still mulling over her words.

She lifted her right brow and that made him answer in a haste, "He was killed six months ago."

Leah waited for more forthcoming information and then sighed. She had to pull it out of him.

"How was he killed, Mark?" she asked patiently.

Her tone showered Mark with cold water and he finally understood that he was supposed to give her more details.

"He was stabbed one night, on the Harbour Front. No witnesses, no clues… The case is still unsolved."

"Where exactly on the Harbour Front?" Leash asked in an edgy voice.

She was close to slapping him silly. Patience wasn't her strong suit.

"Behind that building with the dog's exhibition… I don't remember the name," he shook his head.

"So, he was stabbed less than forty meters from Klavdiya's apartment and you didn't bother to mention it," Leah observed in a voice that chilled Mark to the bone.

"I… I hadn't made the connection," he confessed. "But she couldn't have killed him, could she?" he asked and his eyes bulged, ready to pop out of his head. Mark was smart enough to understand how some things occured and why.

Leah pierced him with her eyes. No, she didn't think that Klavdiya would have bothered to kill the man. The detective imagined that the woman had forgotten about Iuri immediately after she'd discarded him like yesterday's news.

However, the location of the crime made it a too flagrant coincidence and she was compelled to check it further.

"All right, Mark, listen here. Until I finish my lunch and drink my coffee, you call the office and ask that the file related to Iuri's murder is sent to me. I want it in my office this afternoon. You'll also call Anna or Josh and ask them to gather all possible information about Lydia Alder and that spouse of hers, Gareth, but also about George Alder and his father. Have you got that?" she asked icily.

Mark nodded and started making the calls under her glacial eyes. He tried to keep his composure but the slight trembling of his fingers gave him away. Leah's heart tightened noticing his distress but unfortunately, Mark needed a good nudge now and then.

The lieutenant continued munching on her sandwich and, at the same time, she surveyed the detective following her orders. When she finished the last morsel, she wiped her mouth with the napkin that Mark had left on her side of the table and sipping from her coffee, she checked the notes she'd made on her pad.

The last name on their list was Axel Arnett, one of the two people who hadn't bothered to honor Mr. Dimitri Papadopoulos' party with their presence or to excuse themselves.

The first one, a Mr. Tremblay, had been called back to Montreal where he had business and he'd been in such a rush to get there that he didn't have the time to let Mr. Papadopoulos know about his departure. They'd verified and indeed the man had left two days before the crime and never returned.

Arnett lived in one of the exclusive condos on the waterfront. Whether irony, coincidence or fate, his building was not far from Klavdiya's or from the spot where Iuri Grigoriev's torso made the acquaintance of the sharp end of a blade.

The lieutenant's fingers itched with impatience when she read Arnett's name. She sensed that she needed to meet him and as soon as possible. Her anxiety increased a notch, as well as her wish to leave immediately.

She waited for Mark to end his phone conversations and then she signaled him that it was time to go.

When they walked out of the shop they had the feeling that they'd stepped directly into an oven. It was a short distance to Leah's car but the heat almost liquefied their cells. Leah expected to melt any moment now.

Worse, her restlessness amplified and rushed through her veins. She felt compelled to become acquainted with that Mr. Arnett as soon as possible and she disliked the sensation.

Their drive to the waterfront was uneventful, but tedious, and the lieutenant's patience was frayed. Mark kept stealing glances at her trying to assess her mood and that got on her nerves. Still, she couldn't just ask him not to look at her or to control fretting like a scared chicken.

Leah found a spot to park her car at a short distance from the building and braved the heat and humidity with a determined stride.

She didn't look at Mark as she was still upset with him. His indolence rarely jeopardized a case, but chafed at her all the same.

Mark quietly followed her, his eyes on a sail that flirted with the horizon. The knowledge that he'd screwed up big time nudged at him and made him feel uncomfortable in the lieutenant's company.

Sleep was like a love affair for Axel. There were days when he couldn't get enough of it and days when he couldn't run away fast enough.

That day, he'd succumbed to slumber in the wee hours of the morning and he was still blissfully asleep when the front desk called and told him that some police officers were there asking for him.

He scowled and rubbed his eyes. He slid his tongue over his teeth and grimaced.

He pictured the round face of the woman with catlike eyes. He felt threatened somewhat and knew that he had strong reasons for that.

He'd sensed something from her that morning when the police were at the crime scene. Her abilities hadn't been very clear at the time, yet he'd known that he had to remove himself from her proximity.

Apparently, he hadn't removed himself fast enough because she was there now, in his lair, he scowled again. Few people stepped inside his personal space. With a sigh, he asked the reception guy to let them come upstairs.

He couldn't refuse to see them. Their suspicions would have increased tenfold and he would have been called to the police station anyway. Delaying the inevitable wasn't in his nature.

Axel knew that they needed a few minutes to get to his condo and took the time to brush his teeth and pull a pair of pants on.

He'd just grabbed a shirt when he heard the knock on the door and frowned. He'd have liked to be more suitably dressed when they arrived. Clothes were a good armor sometimes. With his shirt in hand, he went to the door and opened it.

Leah's eyes fell on the chest displayed before her eyes and for a few seconds, she just stared. The detective wasn't fond of men that built their body religiously in the gym, but this specimen was something else, and she had a hard time taking her eyes off him.

With effort, she pulled herself together and looked up into the charcoal eyes that burnt on the angular face framed by raven thick hair.

She didn't fail to notice the ironic smile that claimed the corner of the man's mouth. His smile was crooked and gave her the impression that he was mocking her. She narrowed her eyes and her lips pursed.

The man didn't say anything and averted his eyes from hers carefully. He bowed his head in greeting and then stepped aside and waved them inside the apartment.

He closed the door behind them and, like an afterthought, he put his shirt on, but didn't bother to button it. It wasn't as if he hadn't already offered them a show for free and he wasn't very modest.

Axel showed them into his living room, which was almost Spartan. Besides a leather sofa, an armchair and an uncluttered coffee table, nothing else was in plain sight. Even the TV-set was unceremoniously mounted on the wall opposite the sofa but if one didn't look specifically for it, they wouldn't have noticed it.

Apparently, the man didn't care for showing off his means. Leah knew that he had a sizable bank account and several other assets.

The detectives sat down on the black leather sofa although Leah wasn't very comfortable with the idea of sitting there.

The entire scene seemed somewhat unreal. No one had said anything since the moment Axel opened the door. Everything unfolded in complete silence. Mark felt like he was part of the cast in a mute black and white movie and the feeling was unsettling to say the least.

After the officers sat down, Axel headed to the kitchen and, on his way there, he spoke for the first time and asked, "What would you like to drink detectives? I imagine you wouldn't want a beer or a whiskey, as you're on duty, but maybe you'd like a pop."

The sound of his voice startled Leah. She'd listened to the emergency call which the police received in relation to Klavdiya's death. She'd done so repeatedly and she would recognize that voice anywhere and anytime. She had no doubt that it belonged to Axel.

She jumped up ready to go after him and saw his retreating back. From that angle she also recognized the silhouette of the man she'd seen in Mr. Papadopoulos' garden.

Now she understood why she couldn't sense anything from him when he opened the door. She hadn't sensed anything back there in the garden either.

"I'd like you to come back here," she said loudly to his back. "We don't need refreshments. We only need to talk to you," she added and cringed when she heard the edge in her own voice.

"I'm sure you do," his voice came from the kitchen, and then they heard the noise of glasses clattering on a tray and the refrigerator door open. "That's why you're here, I think," he replied loudly.

Mark might have missed a cue now and then, but this time he knew that something was amiss. He also left his seat and came next to Leah taking a defensive position aside her, and that made her smile. The officer seemed ready to protect her and her heart softened towards him.

Leah remembered that there were moments like that that made her like him and even care for him. Mark might have had his weaknesses but he was loyal and dependable when push came to shove.

Axel returned with a big tray piled up with glasses and pop drinks. He stopped just inside the room surprised to see both standing there ready to jump him.

He glanced from one officer to another. His lips twitched, but after a few seconds, he burst into an explosive laughter.

That puzzled the officers and Mark threw out his chest and asked in a belligerent voice, "What's so funny? I don't get it."

Axel stopped, moved the tray to one hand and wiped his eyes with the other. He hadn't laughed like that in a while.

He shook his head and then went to the coffee table and laid the tray there. Turning to them, he said, "You are… I'm just surprised that you didn't have your pistols in hand. That was what was missing," he added snapping his fingers. "Do I really look like the big bad wolf?" he inquired looking at Leah and not without sarcasm.

"Let's sit down," she said softly. "We do have questions for you and you have to explain a few things, mister," she added with a stony face.

"I'm at your disposal, detective," he replied mockingly. "Of course, I'll answer if I can," he thought to make it clear, and after he took a can with orange juice off the tray, he lounged in the armchair. He didn't bother with a glass but drank directly from it.

The detectives stared at him but that didn't disturb him. To her dismay, Leah didn't sense any kind of tension in him, but she couldn't sense anything anyway. The man was like a blank page. There were no thoughts or feelings into which she could delve and that worried her.

Reluctantly, the detectives sat down on the sofa again. The lieutenant grabbed a cold cola off the tray and followed Axel's example. She chose not to use a glass either and she drank directly from the can.

The cold liquid soothed her parched mouth and throat and she sighed contentedly, closing her eyes for a few seconds. After that she glanced swiftly at the two men afraid that they'd heard her.

Mark was drinking a cola as well and seemed in total bliss, as well. Axel's expression was impenetrable.

"Why did you run away when I saw you at the Papadopoulos' house?" she attacked directly.

"I didn't know you wanted to talk to me, detective," Axel answered unconcerned with her directness. "And I didn't run," he pointed out. "If I remember correctly, and, believe me, I do, I just strolled away. If you wanted to talk to me, you could," he observed and sipped from his can again, but he kept his eyes always trained on Leah.

He'd already dismissed Mark. The guy might have been intelligent and might have known his job, but he didn't represent a danger for Axel. Mark had no ESP gift whatsoever and he didn't have a clue about what Axel could do.

Leah, on the other hand, had danger written all over her. Axel guessed that she had a strong gift. She might not have refined it yet, but she knew to use it. He'd felt that in that garden when she tried to probe his mind and he'd also felt it a few minutes earlier when he invited the police officers into his home.

"That's convenient," she remarked tartly.

"What's convenient, detective?" he asked nonplussed.

If she had a hard time to read his mind, so did he with hers. He admitted that he rather liked that, as he'd never met a woman that he couldn't read.

To know every single thought that passed through someone's head got annoying after a while. There was nothing new to discover and he'd found that the unknown held a certain appeal to him.

Axel had enjoyed many women in his lifetime, but lately, he had become increasingly dissatisfied with his romantic life. In the past, he couldn't put his finger on what displeased him, but now, when he became aware that Leah wasn't an open book for him, he understood that he'd been craving for that. He'd longed for something that everybody had but him: the possibility to unwrap layer after layer of a woman's personality and enjoy every new nuance. That was appealing.

"You're the one who called the emergency line," Leah brought him back from his musing. "I recognized your voice, Mr. Arnett," she thought to mention when she noticed his right eyebrow riding up. "If you insist, we can have your voice compared to the recording," she added with nonchalance.

Axel merely shrugged her suggestion away. He knew it was pointless to deny that he'd made that call. Any test would show a one hundred percent match between his voice and the recording that the police had.

He'd thought of that before calling the police to tell them about the murder, but he couldn't just leave that woman there in that garden and not announce her death. It was a matter of conscience.

"So you don't deny," Leah noted and his nonchalant shrug angered her. "All right, explain," she said sharply.

"I can't explain," Axel replied quietly.

"Oh, yes, you can," she answered back with a tough expression on her face.

Axel considered his options and glanced at Mark for a second. He noticed that the man was baffled by the exchange of replies. He didn't understand what was going on and had the feeling that he was missing something important.

"We haven't been introduced," Axel noted and not without a hint of sarcasm.

Leah felt a pinch of guilt. She'd always observed the correct procedure during interviews and yet, this time, she didn't even tell their names to the man.

"I'm Lieutenant Leah MacKay and this is detective Mark Dion," she pointed to Mark.

Axel nodded politely and observed, "I don't suppose you need my name, though. You already know who I am if you are here."

He didn't get a reply to his assumption. The two detectives were just watching him and the silence grew unnerving.

Axel considered his options and leaned forward, bracing his elbows on his knees and said, "I'll tell you everything, lieutenant. But only to you," he added and threw an apologetic glance to Mark. "I apologize, detective, but this is a conversation I'll have only with your lieutenant. It's not for your ears."

Mark frowned and peeked at Leah. She chewed her lower lip for a few seconds, and then said, "That's highly unorthodox."

Axel merely shrugged and noted, "It might be, I don't care. If you don't accept my condition, I won't say anything. Of course, you could charge me with murder, but you will have a hard time proving it. A phone call can be explained away in a hundred ways anyway, but I suppose you want the truth. You can have it but only if we discuss it alone," he stated his position again in a determined voice and Leah understood that there was no other way to make him talk.

They didn't intimidate him and he had the right to keep silent anyway if he chose to.

She turned to Mark and said, "Mark, why don't you go and have another snack? I think there are several cafes and restaurants around here. Bill me afterwards," she added with a smile. "I'll call you when I finish here."

"But, Lieutenant...," the detective started to protest but Leah stopped him with a gesture.

"It'll be fine, Mark. Now, go..." she steered him out of the apartment.

Axel watched him leave and grinned. The detective seemed very reluctant to leave his colleague behind and his hard eyes promised an ocean of pain to Axel if anything happened to Leah.

CHAPTER 7 – A TEMPORARY ALLIANCE

Once the door closed behind Mark, Leah turned to Axel and barked, "Now talk."

"I see that your empathic skills don't extend to your exterior attitude. Politeness isn't one of your strengths," he remarked.

Leah paled under the masked rebuke but repeated stoically, "Talk."

Axel ran his fingers through his thick hair and standing up walked to the window. He looked at the lake without actually seeing anything and reflected about how to start their discussion. It wasn't an easy choice.

Leah had almost lost her last shred of patience and decided to get mean with him, when he turned back to her and eyed her thoughtfully.

"I don't think we should hedge anymore, lieutenant. I know what you are and you know what I am," he said resolutely and yet, in a quiet voice.

"Yes, you're a psychopath," she replied and his eyes flickered with bewilderment.

"I beg your pardon?" he exploded when he finally found his voice.

Leah shrugged and explained without thinking of how it sounded and the consequences of her admission, "All the signs are there. Lack of emotion, no empathy…"

He stopped her by putting up his hand. He shook his head vehemently but she wasn't sure if he denied her assumption or he couldn't believe she'd accuse him like that. She eyed him suspiciously while he rubbed his forehead and massaged his temples.

"So," he began when he found his words again, "you couldn't read me and that led you to the conclusion that I'm a psychopath," he asked for a clarification.

"I don't know what you mean," she retorted, feigning ignorance and her back tensed.

She wanted to bite her tongue. That bit about psychopathy had just slipped out and she was furious with herself.

His mention about reading him didn't sit very well with her. It frightened her that he could be so accurate about what had happened.

"Leah," he started but now she stopped him by copying his gesture from before.

"Either lieutenant or lieutenant Mac-Kay. We're not friends, Arnett, and I don't fraternize with suspects."

He nodded and grinned sarcastically at her.

"I see, *Lieutenant*," he said. "Well, let me alleviate your fears, then. You have to keep an open mind though or otherwise it won't work," he warned her.

"Just talk, Arnett," she snapped at him and both his eyebrows climbed up his forehead when he heard her tone.

"All right. So, *Lieutenant*, I am aware that you can read people's minds and feel-ings. I don't know how well you can do that, but you can and don't try to deny it," he stopped her denial when she opened her mouth. "You tried to read me that day in the garden and you couldn't. I left because I was afraid that you'd have been able to if you'd insisted. However, my leaving didn't mean that I was involved in the crime," he admonished her and she scowled at him.

"What's all this crap about reading people's minds? Either you partied too much last night and aren't yourself now or you're not quite all there, Arnett," she observed and not without irony.

Yet, she was scared. She didn't know how he could be so close to the truth. She hadn't done anything until then to lead him to that assumption and he appeared to know everything.

Axel scrutinized her and shook his head in regret. He burrowed his hands in the pockets of his pants and returned to the window.

Leah had the feeling that he'd simply shut her out and bit her lip. She was rattled and didn't know how to react.

It wasn't as if she'd been confronted with such a situation every day. That angered her and she searched for the most biting words she could throw at him.

Yet, she didn't have a chance to do so because he began talking again although his voice sounded tired.

"We are the same, you and I... Or almost the same. You can read minds and feelings, lieutenant. I can read minds but I'm not very attuned to people's feelings," he shrugged as if that lack of his had been insignificant. "But I have visions," he added and turned to face her. "It's not something enjoyable, as you can imagine," he said bitterly.

She opened her mouth to squash his assumption that she had such abilities but he shook his head stubbornly.

"Don't bother," he said. "What's the point?" he opened his arms.

She relented and tilting her head, she observed him attentively.

"You mean to say that you had a vision with the crime and that's why you called," she assumed.

"Yes, that's what I'm saying," he replied harshly. "Actually, everything began while I was sleeping. When I woke up, I wasn't even sure whether I'd had a nightmare or a vision but then I saw the continuation of the events while awake so I had to assume that it was a vision... I know very well my friend's house and garden, so I recognized them and of course, it was easy for me to pinpoint the crime scene," he explained and crossed his arms across his chest.

"Why didn't you go to the party? You were invited," she thought to inquire, as she wasn't very convinced he was telling the truth.

"I didn't feel like it," he shrugged. "Dimitri and I don't care about such niceties, so I didn't bother to excuse myself. Anyways, I knew he'd have enough people there to make up for my absence," he observed with indifference.

Leah stared at him with impassive eyes for a few seconds. She'd have liked to refute his assumptions but she knew very well that skills like his were real. There were a few people in her family who exhibited them and she couldn't deny the validity of his claim. She thought that she'd better put to good use what he'd seen and stopped pretending it was all just balderdash.

"I imagine you saw more than just the body on the ground," she went out on a limb.

He nodded. "Yes, I saw almost everything. I mean I saw the victim flirting with a big man. After some banter, which I couldn't hear but things appeared that way, they went out in the garden. They strolled leisurely until they got to the far end and there he grabbed her and dragged her to the place where you found her. He ripped her blouse – I remember she was thinking about that blouse. It was a symbol for her. It encompassed everything she'd achieved," he explained with large gestures and stopped for a moment.

Axel returned to the armchair and sat down after snatching another can of juice. He tapped the can with practiced efficiency and swallowed all the liquid in short order.

He looked back at Leah and said, "I can't hear what people say in my visions. I see only their lips moving and I have a general feeling about what's what. That's how I know about the flirting, for instance. Yet, I can read their thoughts," he specified. "Like that piece about the blouse…

That woman was very fond of it. She really loved that top… At the beginning, she was dismayed because the blouse had been ruined and only afterwards she realized she was in danger…," he shook his head as if he couldn't believe it. "Anyway, the woman was a feisty little thing. She fought that guy and who knows, she might have survived but two more came," he continued with regret.

Axel told her every excruciating detail of the crime he'd witnessed and only when he'd exhausted all the specifics, did he stop talking.

Leah looked at him and saw the signs of tiredness etched on his face. Fine lines had appeared around his eyes and they hadn't been there when they came to see him that afternoon.

"It must have been awful to witness that and feel powerless," she observed quietly.

Axel looked at her and chuckled bitterly, "You have no idea."

He rubbed his face with his palms and continued, "The problem is that I don't know how you can use what I've told you. Yes, you'll have detailed descriptions of the three attackers. At least that much it is true. The problem is that you won't find them in the victim's regular circle. They were hired hands," he pointed out.

"You're sure of that," she asked for confirmation.

"Yes, I am," he restated. "I've told you that I can read thoughts even if I can't hear the words when I have a vision... After they killed her, one of them, the one who brought her to that isolated corner, thought that they had a lot of fun and made 30 k each in the process... One of them, the thin one, didn't seem so exhilarated, though. I know that he hesitated whenever it was his turn to plant the knife in that woman."

Leah reflected upon his words and said, "All right. I have their general descriptions, although I'd like you to work with an artist so that I could get detailed portraits. I also know that someone paid 90 k for her murder. That helps, I think."

"Maybe...," Axel expressed his skepticism. "You know, I've told you about that guy... How he thought about the money and the fun..."

Leah nodded and leaned forward. She had the feeling that he had something important to say but didn't know how.

"The thought read like this: '*She'll be satisfied with what she got in exchange for the 30 k apiece and we had fun in the process*'," Axel remembered. "I don't think the victim would have paid them that amount of money to rape and torture her," he observed. "Another woman must have been involved."

"Right," Leah agreed and frowned. She reflected on the words and said, "It means that another woman paid the money to have Klavdiya murdered. Considering how she asked the murder to be done, she must have hated the victim badly."

Axel nodded and stood up. "I need some food, lieutenant. Would you mind if we move to the kitchen?" he inquired.

Leah hesitated. It was out of the ordinary to conduct an interview in a kitchen while the witness was having a snack but then the entire interview hadn't followed regulations so far. She nodded and followed him.

"Would you care for some bacon and eggs? I'm too famished to think of making something else right now," he explained and opened the fridge door to take out the ingredients for the meal.

"No, thank you," she replied, "I just had lunch before coming here."

"I see," he said softly, and his voice brought a frown on her face.

"I didn't mean anything by that, Arnett. I've just eaten and I won't eat twice just to spare your feelings," she specified.

He laughed and shook his head, "You're the first empath I've ever seen who doesn't spare people's feelings. You're a walking contradiction, lieutenant."

She didn't care for his assumption and retorted testily, "We'll have a working collaboration, Arnett, nothing more. Although I'll have to find a way to use what you saw and what you know without revealing the other stuff. People will say we're crazy and that's a label I could live without," she ended her tirade by poking his chest with her finger repeatedly.

"Ouch, lieutenant. That's one bony finger and it hurts when you do that," he said with amusement in his voice and rubbed the spot she'd poked.

He put a pan on the stove and threw the bacon inside to fry and turned to Leah again.

They assessed each other for a few seconds and then the man said, "Now, don't tell me, detective, that you haven't thought of me at all. You must have been at least somewhat intrigued when you couldn't read my mind."

"I was worried not intrigued," she corrected him. "I was convinced you were a psychopath," she reminded him.

"Oh, yes, so you've said," he whispered. "Nonetheless, now you know the truth," he pointed out.

"So?" she inquired.

"Well, I'm intrigued," he confessed.

"Let me say this again," she said. "So?"

"Considering that I haven't been intrigued in a woman for a long time, you can't think that I'd let this chance just go away," he replied.

"Not interested," she retorted with feigned indifference.

"Do people believe your lies?" he wondered keeping his eyes steady on her.

His question ruffled her feathers and she almost growled. Leah was good at hiding her real feelings and wasn't a bad liar either. His astute observation irritated her because she was interested in him indeed and she disliked the fact that he was aware of that.

She'd been fascinated when she laid her eyes on him for the first time, even though she'd had only a glimpse of the man lying underneath those handsome features. Yet, after talking to him and being in his presence for some time, she found it difficult to dismiss his magnetism.

"I don't know what you're talking about. Cook your... breakfast," she ordered. "We have things to do."

Axel mused and turned to the stove to flip the bacon over. He didn't forget to reply though, "I'm a civilian, Lieutenant, and I don't have to take orders from you, remember?"

Leah's irritation reached a new high and she imagined herself snatching the pan off the stove and slamming it over his head with a resounding bang. That fantasy was satisfactory enough and her tension subsided.

Axel, always with his back at her, grinned. When the fury took the best of her, she couldn't guard her thoughts from him as before and he succeeded in reading what she was thinking.

Her little stint with the pan amused him enough. He also appreciated her gutsy nature.

Leah, on the other hand, wasn't able to penetrate his thoughts. She sensed his amusement and yet, she didn't know why he felt that way. Her inability to read his feelings frustrated her to no end.

The woman didn't like it when her own limitations stopped her from doing something. She needed to do something else so that she could take her mind off that failure.

"I'm going to make some calls until you finish making your… lunch," she supplied, unsure what she could call his meal. "I'll send Mark to the office to check on some things," she continued and he shrugged with indifference.

He didn't care what she did with the information he'd given her. He knew she wouldn't reveal how he'd obtained that information because then she'd have to come forward and admit that she believed in ESP.

He didn't think she'd ever do that. Keeping a reputation in the police force as a woman was not an easy task even though progress had brought new standards around.

However, admitting to something that people either dismissed with ignorance or were attracted to like to a freaky curiosity would have led to the end of her career and she loved her profession. She was far too invested in it not to protect it at all costs.

CHAPTER 8 – BEWARE OF A WOMAN SCORNED AND A MAN'S BRUISED EGO

Axel watched the interview with interest. His eyes were on Leah though.

He wasn't interested in observing the sturdy man who was trying to talk his way out of a murder charge. Leah could do that without his help and anyway, it wasn't like he couldn't hear his thoughts.

He was more interested in Leah's demeanor and in her ability to hide what she thought or felt under a blank mask. Axel couldn't discern if she was frustrated or disappointed.

Everyone had expected to have serious problems making the man who lured Klavdiya into the isolated area of the garden talk, but they'd been wrong. The man was singing away, eager to offer them all possible details. He hoped for some leniency when the case would go to court.

Axel shook his head bewildered. He couldn't believe that that man harbored such expectations. He hadn't only raped and killed a woman for money, but he'd deeply enjoyed every torture he inflicted on her.

Axel considered that it wasn't enough if they locked him up and threw the key away. At times like this, he regretted that Canada didn't have capital punishment.

He knew that Mark was in the other interrogation room and together with Anne, who Axel had just met, questioned another of the trio, the thin man who'd appeared reluctant to do his part of the job during the night of the murder.

Leah didn't have too much difficulty finding the three men. Although they hadn't been on Dimitri's guest list, they'd been the only ones in Toronto who, within the last two weeks, deposited 30 k each in the bank.

Axel shook his head. He couldn't believe that people could be so stupid sometimes. He didn't understand how those men could have thought that depositing such a large amount of money wouldn't raise eyebrows. Moreover, all of them had opened accounts and deposited the money at the same bank and at the same time.

Leah picked them up immediately and, ironically enough, the toughest of all couldn't spill the beans fast enough. The other two showed more restraint, though. They didn't confess to anything until they'd been shown some sort of proof.

Axel's head snapped to the door of the interrogation room where someone had just knocked. Leah closed the file she had open before her on the desk and, taking it with her, she left the room.

Axel hurried from his observation post and joined her outside just in time to hear a policeman in uniform saying, "Yes, he's here and asked to speak to that man," he pointed to the interrogation room with his chin.

Axel frowned and glanced at Leah. She pondered the news and then went back into the interrogation room after she asked the officer to wait for a few moments.

When she returned, Axel was leaning back on the wall, his arms crossed over his chest. She spoke directly to the officer, without sparing a glance at him.

"Please, bring the counsel here. I will let the others know."

The officer went back to the reception area and Leah tapped her foot furiously on the floor. She was beyond mad although her face didn't show it.

"What happened, lieutenant?" Axel approached her.

"They've got counsel," she said succinctly and headed to the interrogation room where Mark was with one of the other suspects.

"How come?" Axel asked. "I haven't heard them asking for one and at least that guy in there with you confessed to a lot of things already," he noticed.

"Don't you think I know that?" she whirled back to him.

Now, he noticed that she was beyond furious. Her catlike eyes threw daggers and her skin was taut over her cheekbones.

"I don't know how someone knew to send a counsel for them, but I'll find out," she said and her tone promised nothing good.

"At least you've found out how they got to Dimitri's party," Axel noticed trying to change her mood. "Dimitri won't be pleased when he finds out that he has such disloyal people on the payroll and he has to change the lot of them."

"Look," Leah stopped and turned to him with blank eyes. "I think you should go home. There's nothing more that you could do here."

Axel tried to say something but she touched his chest and whispered, "Please."

He gnashed his teeth and looked away from her but, after a brief reflection, he decided to respect her decision. He knew she had a lot to deal with right then and he didn't want to add more to her burden.

Axel glanced back at her and said sternly, "I'll go now, lieutenant, but you know where to find me."

Leah nodded and then hurried to Mark's interrogation room to stop his interview as well. She didn't want to think of the implication of Axel's words. She pushed them to the back of her mind to analyze them later.

Axel was looking out of the window pensively when he heard the knock on the door. His eyebrows raised. No one ever came upstairs without his agreement and the front desk hadn't called to let him know that he had visitors.

He considered going and unlocking the door but didn't feel like entertaining visitors. Then the knock became insistent and the thought that Leah came to visit him crossed his mind.

That was the only explanation. The front desk guy might have allowed her to come upstairs if she'd showed him her ID and asked him not to call the apartment.

Axel unlocked the door and reached for the handle to open it when the door was slammed into his head with force and he was thrown into the opposite wall. When he hit the wall, his brain suffered a second concussion and he lost consciousness.

Axel came back to reality when cold water was splashed all over his face. He sputtered and opened his eyes. The light coming from the bulb just above him hurt his eyes and he closed them with a hiss.

"Oh, no, you don't," he heard a screech, and a pointy shoe kicked him in his ribs and stole his breath for a few moments.

He tried to see who was in the apartment with him and half-opened his eyes. His mind was muddled and he couldn't focus enough to read his attacker's mind.

When he tried to brace his hand on the floor so that he could stand, he realized that he was trussed like a turkey. The rope around his hands and legs was tight and didn't give way to his efforts.

When Axel swore viciously, a maniacal laugh joined his words and two small hands sealed his mouth with adhesive tape.

"Bring him here," Leah asked Josh and crossed her hands on the desk.

Her blue-green eyes shot lightning bolts and Mark didn't dare to interrupt her thoughts.

Since the legal counsel showed for the three suspects, Leah had hurled them all into a whirlwind of activity. She wanted to know how the counselor received word to come because the three men had declined counsel from the beginning.

As they'd arrested them in the apartment they shared and no one was the wiser, the only explanation Leah could accept was that someone in the squad room had leaked the word outside. She asked them to check all the calls made on the floor and cross-reference them with all the people they had on the suspect list.

It wasn't easy or fast to check so many calls and Leah's frustration increased with every minute that passed. Everyone walked on eggshells around the lieutenant and avoided making eye contact with her.

They knew that Leah was afraid that the call might have been made from a cell phone or from outside the building. In that situation, they couldn't trace it and couldn't find the leak. More than one case could be in jeopardy.

Josh was the lucky one. He tracked a call made at exactly five minutes after they started the interrogations. The phone number that was dialed matched the cell phone number they had for Gareth.

Now Leah wanted to have a word with him. The last time she talked to him, he seemed very open and expressed sadness and shock when he heard that Klavdiya had been killed. At the time, she sensed that regret and sorrow, but she also sensed a bruised ego.

At the same time, she wanted to chat with the officer that had betrayed his uniform and that before sending his file to the internal affairs commission. The Chief had approved the interview because he knew that she had a murder case to solve.

As Josh went to bring Gareth in and she knew that it might take a while before he came back, Leah decided to begin with the officer who had made the call.

Leah thought that she should interview him in an interrogation room to show him that the situation was serious. She also wanted the interview to take place in the presence of two other officers so that no complains could be raised later. Hence, she invited Mark and a Sargent from the Squad to assist her in the interview.

When she entered the interrogation room, the young officer who was waiting for the interview to begin stood up. His hands were shaking and the pastiness of his face showed that he was terrified.

Leah waved him to sit down and Mark and the Sargent sat next to her. She recited the date and the names of the people in the room for the video tape and then, she leaned forward.

"Do you know why you're in this room?" she asked the officer.

The young man shook his head and licked his lips. He hid his hands in his lap.

Leah had already noticed that his fingers were shaking visibly but didn't feel any compassion for him.

"Do you remember that you called Gareth Black three hours ago?"

The man glanced from one interrogator to another. He muttered something under his breath, but the officers couldn't make out the words.

Leah sensed his fear. The man couldn't gather his thoughts and was instinctively looking for a way out.

"Paul," she called him by his first name.

Her quiet voice penetrated the haze of his panic and he looked up at her.

"Calm down now, all right. You've made a serious mistake. That's true. Don't compound your mistake with another," she pleaded looking straight into his eyes.

Her voice soothed the young man and his anxiety subdued. He wiped his face and breathed deeply.

"I'll tell you everything," he suddenly decided. "Lydia, Gareth's wife, is my cousin… She's… special… She's always had a strange look upon the world… She thinks that she deserves everything and no one has the right to refuse her what she wants… Her parents encouraged that streak… Probably because they were afraid… I don't know… Anyways, if she perceives something like an attack against her… no matter how insignificant, she re-acts… Detective," he said turning to Leah and addressing her directly, "to be honest, I'm afraid of her. I know how mean she could get when we were children… My parents asked my uncle to have her seen

by a doctor if not committed, but he refused… Now, two days ago, Gareth came
and told me that she'd hired three guys to
beat up a woman who tried to lure him
into her bed… Just to beat her… But they
went overboard and killed that woman…
I believed him… or I wanted to believe
him," he chose to be honest. "I wanted to
believe him because I was afraid. When he
asked me to let him know if there was any
arrest in this specific case, he also told me
that Lydia would be grateful to me if I
helped her. If not… He didn't say what
Lydia would do but everyone in the family knows what she can do… She's sneaky
and got away with a lot of things along the
time… I have a baby, lieutenant…," the officer said and his eyes shimmered.
"Gareth told me to think of my baby girl…
I know Lydia and I didn't want her to hurt
my child. She wouldn't do it right now,
but maybe tomorrow or the day after tomorrow… She once waited for five years
to take her revenge…"

"All right, Paul, I understand that,"
Leah said.

She did understand him and she sensed that his distress and fear were genuine. She didn't understand why he hadn't come to her when Gareth asked him to snitch for him, but that was another matter altogether.

"Tell me what information you gave to Gareth," she asked him quietly.

Leah, Anne and Mark drove as fast as possible to Axel's address. An intervention car accompanied them. They wanted to be ready for anything.

When Leah heard that Gareth had been informed about Axel's involvement, she knew that Axel would be on Lydia's revenge list. She'd had one for the last thirty years, apparently.

As far as everybody knew, Axel had stumbled onto the crime scene that night, seen the three attackers right after they killed the woman, and had run away to call the police.

Leah explained to the Chief that he hadn't waited near the crime scene because the men were still there. He was alone and couldn't fight three men armed with knives.

The Chief accepted the explanation and Axel's written testimony, which would throw the three men in prison for the remainder of their life.

They couldn't be sure that Lydia would act so quickly after finding out his name and address but they couldn't leave anything to chance. The young officer had given every piece of information to Gareth and when they spoke to him, Gareth confessed that he'd already passed it on to Lydia.

He'd also told them that she had a way inside Axel's building. She had a friend who lived there and she could pretend to visit her at any time. The front desk people knew her and wouldn't ask her where she was going.

Gareth had been very talkative once he realized that he had no chance to go back to his luxurious life. He had a lot of things to say but Leah didn't bother to wait around. She left Josh in charge of the interview and assembled a team to go to Axel's house immediately.

They didn't park the cars when they got to the building but left them in the street. They rushed inside and the man from the front desk immediately opened the door to the elevator when he saw policemen in uniform. He didn't even ask them where they wanted to go.

When they exited the elevator, Leah signaled them to be quiet and they tiptoed to Axel's door. She led the way and leaned on the wall on the side of the door when she saw that Axel's door was open.

Leah waved the officers to stand down and she took her pistol out of the holster. She checked to see that it was working properly and then she entered the apartment.

Her mind was assaulted by a turbulence of emotions. She could read anger, frustration, hate, anguish and triumph. It was a cacophony of feelings that pointed to emotional disequilibrium and that made her believe that Lydia wouldn't stop just because she saw the police.

When Paul told them about Lydia's special emotional state, she'd thought that he exaggerated because he wanted to explain his actions. Now, she understood that she'd been wrong. That was a woman capable of anything.

Leah breathed deeply and entered the apartment. She heard a muffled shout from the living room and headed towards the sound.

When she reached the living room, she saw Axel thoroughly bound on the floor and Lydia leaning over him. She had a knife in her right hand and, apparently, she'd used it a couple of times on Axel's body.

Leah wasn't able to assess Axel's condition from that distance. She could see blood stains on his arms, legs and chest but she had no means of determining how serious his wounds were.

"Lydia," she called out to the woman who'd just raised the knife to stab Axel again.

Lydia turned around with a yelp. Her beautiful features were contorted from rage and the dilation of her pupils showed that she was beyond normal comprehension.

"Step back," Leah ordered her.

Lydia looked at her and then at Axel. With a snicker, she prepared to plunge the blade of the knife into Axel again.

"Put the knife down," Leah repeated with more authority but Lydia didn't heed her warning and raised her arm to drive the blade with more force in the body lying at her feet.

Leah didn't repeat the warning. She shot Lydia's hand and the bullet went through one side of her palm into the other.

A howl of pain erupted from the woman's lips and she curled on the floor whimpering.

She didn't seem to understand what had happened and Leah read her frantic thoughts with clarity. Lydia had no memory of what she'd been doing there. She knew only that she was hurt and in pain.

Leah called Mark to take her away and she rushed to Axel's side.

EPILOGUE

When Leah entered his apartment, she heard the noise of a football game on the TV and she shook her head. Axel should have been in bed.

She'd had to fight him to make him remain in the hospital for two days and she relented afterwards only because he'd promised to rest.

"That's not resting," she said in a dry voice.

Axel turned his head from the screen and grinned at her, "Football is always relaxing for a man, Leah, didn't you know?"

Leah pursed her lips but she couldn't be upset with him. After he'd been stabbed five times and survived, he had the right to spend his time with the things he loved.

She came to the sofa where he lounged and put the bag with Chinese food on the coffee table.

"Brought you some lunch," she said and without realizing it, her fingers brushed a lock of raven hair off his face.

Axel watched her with serious eyes and then he took her hand in his. He looked at the hand that had saved his life and then, he leaned his cheek in her palm.

Leah felt strange. She stared at his face and closed her eyes and tried to read his mind to see what he was thinking but she couldn't. She saw contentment on his face and that was the only thing she could be sure about.

"Would you like to eat, stranger?" she asked him softly.

He nodded, at the same time nuzzling her palm, and electrical shocks ran up her arm. She tried to stand up and they played a game of tug of war with her hand.

Leah couldn't stop a merry laugh and she pushed him gently back. He fell on his back and said, "You'll come back, you know."

She nodded and smiling went to the kitchen to bring what they needed to share the food.

"So, did you close the case?" Axel asked and forked some more chicken into his mouth.

Leah nodded, chewed and then she said, "Actually, I closed two cases."

"Do tell," Axel said and sat straighter.

"That Iuri Gregoriev... You heard about him...," she looked at him inquiringly and Axel bobbed his head in agreement. "Well, Lydia killed him too. She wanted us to arrest Klavdiya and she tried to plant some evidence, but the officer in charge of the investigation didn't even look in Klavdiya's direction. That was why Lydia decided that she had to make her pay in another way."

"I understand that the killers got into Dimitri's house because they paid some guards. What I don't understand is how they knew she'd be there," Axel frowned.

"Simple. The guy that Klavdiya had just met... George Adler paid him to pick her up, charm her and invite her to the party. The man was in dire financial straits and needed every cent he could make," she explained.

Axel shook his head in puzzlement. He knew that guy. Not very well, but well enough. He'd never have expected him to approve of such a scheme.

"So, you closed the files," he murmured watching her carefully.

"Yep," she said and picked up her can of cola and sipped.

"Then, you don't need me anymore," he observed.

She shook her head and something fluttered in his heart. It tasted like regret.

"I see," he said and left the food on the table. "Excuse me a moment," he said and stood up with difficult to go onto the balcony. He needed some fresh air because his throat hurt.

"I'll come with you," she said. "You owe me your life, remember," she joked. "I have to keep a close eye on you from now on," she added.

He turned to her and for the first time since they met she saw emotion in his eyes. He slid his good arm around her

back and crushed her to his chest. Leah
didn't imagine he'd have so much
strength after all that stabbing and bleed-
ing.

Also by Roxana Nastase:

Mayhem on Nightingale Street (Book 1 – McNamara Series)

Forthcoming:

Scents and Shadows (Book 2 – McNamara Series)

A Churchgoing Woman

An Immigrant

Thank you for taking the time to read the novel **A Suitable Epitaph**.

If you enjoyed it, please consider telling your friends or posting a short review. Word of mouth is an author's best friend and much appreciated.

Thank you, Roxana Nastase.

www.ingramcontent.com/pod-product-compliance
Lightning Source LLC
Chambersburg PA
CBHW070507200726
48293CB00007B/2420